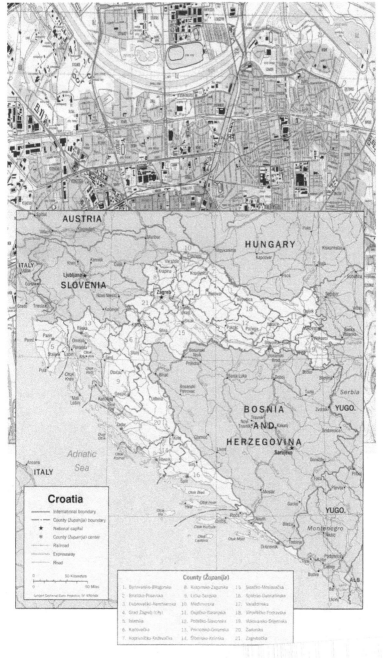

Croatia

- International boundary
- County (Županija) boundary
- ★ National capital
- ◉ County (Županija) center
- Railroad
- Expressway
- Road

0   50 Kilometers
0   50 Miles

Lambert Conformal Conic Projection, SP. 43°N/44N

County (Županija)

1. Bjelovarsko-Bilogorsko	8. Krapinsko-Zagorsko	15. Sisačko-Moslavačka
2. Brodsko-Posavska	9. Ličko-Senjska	16. Splitsko-Dalmatinske
3. Dubrovačko-Neretvanska	10. Međimurska	17. Varaždinska
4. Grad Zagreb (city)	11. Osječko-Baranjska	18. Virovitičko-Podravska
5. Istarska	12. Požeško-Slavonska	19. Vukovarsko-Srijemska
6. Karlovačka	13. Primorsko-Goranska	20. Zadarska
7. Koprivničko-Križevačka	14. Šibensko-Kninska	21. Zagrebačka

Croatia

- International boundary
- County (Županija) boundary
- ★ National capital
- ⊕ County (Županija) center
- Railroad
- Expressway
- Road

0   50 Kilometers
0   50 Miles

Lambert Conformal Conic Projection, SP standards

County (Županija)

1. Bjelovarsko-Bilogorska
2. Brodsko-Posavska
3. Dubrovačko-Neretvanska
4. Grad Zagreb (city)
5. Istarska
6. Karlovačka
7. Koprivničko-Križevačka
8. Krapinsko-Zagorski
9. Ličko-Senjska
10. Međimurska
11. Osječko-Baranjska
12. Požeško-Slavonska
13. Primorsko-Goranska
14. Šibensko-Kninska
15. Sisačko-Moslavačka
16. Splitsko-Dalmatinska
17. Varaždinska
18. Virovitičko-Podravska
19. Vukovarsko-Srijemska
20. Zadarska
21. Zagrebačka

Zagreb, Exit South

ZAGREB, EXIT SOUTH

edo popović

translated by julienne eden bušić

OOLIGAN
PRESS

ISBN13: 978-1-932010-09-1

This book was previously published in the Croatian language as
Izlaz Zagreb jug © Meander (Zagreb, Croatia), 2003.

Original English translation by Julienne Eden Bušić.

Publication of this work is partially underwritten by a grant
from the Ministry of Culture of the Republic of Croatia.

Author photo by Ivan Posavec
Maps courtesy of the University of Texas Libraries,
The University of Texas at Austin.
For full credits, see back matter.

Ooligan Press
Portland State University
PO Box 751
Portland, OR 97207-0751
ooligan@ooliganpress.pdx.edu
www.ooligan.pdx.edu

ZAGREB, EXIT SOUTH

1. Fear of going home and the dying out of domestic beer

Imagine that an aircraft carrier is passing right in front of your nose, ejecting those deafeningly loud things that explode in the air. Or that a bunch of right-wing radical chicks (who, by the way, put out for free) are lined up on the sidewalk in minis and fishnet stockings, agitating for the social rights of Afro-Asian immigrant prostitutes. Or that the Pope and Fidel Castro are dancing the rumba in your living room. And you don't even react, you don't even notice. Because all your capacities, all your nerve endings and little gray cells, every hair follicle is focused on something momentous. Really momentous.

The finals of the soccer World Cup, for example, and your team is losing, but they've set up their line, they're squeezing the adversary, a goal is hanging in the air, it's a madhouse, and then your TV craps out. And you just sit there, gaping at that fucking box in disbelief.

Throw a bottle at it.

Throw it out the window.

Throw yourself out the window.

What to do?

This is what your brain is focused on; it's not interested in anything else.

Here's Baba's situation. He's sitting at the computer in the Agramer press office and staring at the monitor with that crapped-out TV look on his face. Just gaping at that empty Microsoft screen waiting for some miracle to happen. For the Holy Virgin of Software to appear and speak one sentence, one simple lousy sentence, and then he'd be okay. No problem. He just needs that first sentence.

Everything had seemed so simple that morning. So insanely simple. Driving to work, he'd had a story, the first sentence, a few great scenes, everything. Now all he had was an endless virtual roll of paper, and an empty screen with nothing behind it.

"Is everything okay?"

Baba, startled, turned and looked up. Those voices that all of a sudden echo out from somewhere. Like when God called out to Abraham about Isaac. Fortunately, God rarely called on Baba. And this time was no exception. A journalist from the City news section was standing next to Baba's desk. She'd only been working there a few weeks and still hadn't quite gotten the hang of it. Didn't have a clue what she had fallen into. Thought the section editor was screwing her out of love, and that all the gastritic, surly, bloated veterans with the bloodshot eyes, like Baba, were "colorful characters." Thought they were cool. Not realizing that a few years down the road, she'd be "colorful," too. And would definitely not be thinking of herself as cool.

"Can I help you?" Baba asked, pulling himself together.

"Piece of junk," she said. "My computer's frozen up, too."

"The computer's fine," said Baba.

"Maybe you should try to reboot it anyway."

"The problem is here," Baba said, tapping his finger against his temple.

"You can restart that, too," she said.

"Maybe," he answered. "How about it?"

"What?"

"How about a drink," Baba suggested. "Reboot the system, whatever."

"I've got to go write," she said.

"Of course," he said, "Why didn't I think of that?"

The café terrace in front of the newsroom was swarming with journalists. They were loud-talking, laughing, drinking their drinks. Some called Baba over to join them. He waved them off and went on toward the parking lot. He was still plagued by that nebulous sentence. *Shit, I should have stopped somewhere this morning on the side of the road and written it down. Now it's too late.* How many times had he lost something, thinking: I'll do it later. Tomorrow. There's plenty of time. But those kinds of things don't wait for you forever. They're always on the move. They take their twists and turns, only rarely crossing paths with you.

That woman you passed on the street the other day, you'll probably never meet her again. She smiled at you as though she knew you, you could have greeted her, started a conversation, and who knows what would have come of it—but nothing. You hesitated too long, and when you turned back, she was already lost in the crowd. You've got to be quick when things like that are concerned. Grab them first and think about what you're going to do with them later. Dinosaurs are extinct because they didn't think fast enough. Just munching on their leaves and branches and telling themselves, there's plenty of time. Only Eternity's got plenty of time, you know?

Baba was driving along Slavonska Avenue, heading east, thinking about where to go. *Home? No way, definitely not home.* Home was depressing. He went by the Croatian Television complex and turned north and then down Miramarska Street to the city center. He drove around the city for a while trying to set some destination point. It was always the same scene—houses left and right, and between them, blinking traffic signals. It got boring driving around in circles. He couldn't decide where to go. Couldn't think of a single place that seemed tempting. What could that special place possibly be, anyhow, at four o'clock in the afternoon, in Zagreb, in the middle of summer? Waiting for the green light across from St. Vincent Church, he checked out the building facades facing Ilica Street, fantasizing about something happening. That a tram was traveling down the street. That the crane hovering above those roofs collapsed. That somebody burst out of a door with a Kalashnikov and opened fire on the passersby.

Nothing happened. He turned into Dalmatinska Street and parked.

Baba wished he could go home. Take off his loafers, give Vera the obligatory kiss, open a cold beer, stretch out on the couch, and tell her about his day.

Tell her how a cat, lurking in the bushes by the student dormitories, caught a sparrow and ate it.

And about the woman who fainted on the sidewalk near Gundulić Street, and then the passersby hopping over her or simply going around.

Or the old guy, watching the wind twirling a plastic bag around in the air, saying, "It's all so fornicating simple!"

Meanwhile, Baba can't go home and tell Vera about the cat, the woman, or the old man. Not just because these are old stories he told her long ago. That's not the problem. The problem is that Vera's waiting for him with that mute, rigid look that acts upon him like an electroshock.

Actually, Vera DOESN'T EVEN LOOK at Baba when he comes home. She EVALUATES him. Evaluates the elasticity of his footsteps. How bent his knees are. Whether he's reaching for the wall. What angle his body is to the ground.

Vera also doesn't listen anymore to what Baba says, just whether he's speaking from the throat or from the diaphragm.

Baba enters the apartment more and more frequently stepping stiffly, knees barely bending, bombed to the gills. Bellows out a greeting from deep in the gut. Hand groping in panic for the wall.

"Jesus," he mumbles, "what a nightmare day I had."

Or, "Ever since this morning, my head's been killing me, like the top's going to blow off."

Or, "Something I ate in the cafeteria didn't agree with me."

Or something similar.

And Vera turns her head away from him. Doesn't say anything, just loses herself in her own thoughts. And Baba drags himself over to the couch and starts expounding on some big plans he has. Jabbering about some novel he's going to write. Or how another department wants him and is offering him a big raise. Or how nowadays there isn't even…

Vera's not listening to him. Her ears are losing the capacity to pick up Baba's frequency. And he's losing himself in a labyrinth of unconnected thoughts. And then he falls asleep.

When he wakes up, he tries to bring up some inconsequential topic, just checking out the terrain. Observes Vera, attempting to reconstruct what happened when he came home. Was he talking a bunch of shit? Did he go off on her verbally? Was she even home when he came in? He blathers on about something trivial, looking at Vera with the eyes of a boxer forced into the corner. And Vera's silent, and he can't read on her face what she's thinking. That's why Baba is so fucking afraid to go home. Fear of going home is an unresearched illness. For some inexplicable reason it's been neglected and, in contrast to other fears, has no medical status whatsoever. It doesn't even have a name. How do you cure yourself of an unnamed illness, ignored by the medical world? And that's why Baba is standing at the counter of the Komiža buffet in Masarykova Street, still in his loafers, silently drinking his lukewarm beer, and thinking about the things a guy who's afraid to go home always thinks about.

"Oh, heart of the city, what youth you've blessed me with." The words of an old hit song were crackling out of a wall speaker, and Baba, wiping foam from his lips with the palm of his hand, was thinking about how the old dive was still resisting the merciless blows of "innovation." What does that mean? Most of all, it means that in the Komiža buffet you could still get domestic beer. And that's not an insignificant thing if you give it a little thought. As an unenlightened anti-globalist—and because it was totally clear to him that the joke about the October Revolution and the vodka wasn't really a joke—Baba didn't really care about the avalanche of "advancements" that had bombarded Zagreb after the fall of the Iron Curtain. Ten years later, Baba concluded, when you added up all the pluses and minuses, the only thing worth mentioning was that there were fewer cafés where you could get domestic beer. It turned out that this legendary democracy everyone was talking about consisted of domestic beer getting fucked over.

So Baba was infinitely surprised, (and pleased), that the Komiža still existed in its present form, with its circular counter resembling a bunker, and its chrome surface kept shiny by the elbows of scores of notorious scam artists, the hanging shelf with the hard liquor above the counter, and the glass cabinet (baloney sandwiches embellished with mayonnaise and wilted lettuce leaves). The wooden stools and ceramic tiles on the walls, a hanging lamp of fake crystal. And a bathroom with a stench that would stun a rhino, toilet always plugged up, the cracked urinals, floors slick with piss—but WITHOUT those fascist signs showing a cigarette with a slash across it. And, finally, there was the pudgy barmaid in a white blouse and dark blue skirt, wearing on her swollen feet those faded, ergonomically correct shoes with the toes and ankles cut out. And did she know how to take orders! Coffee? OK. Tea? Indian or rosehip? Ožujsko beer? Sure thing. Wine with mineral water. Grasevina or Riesling? Cognac. Coming right up. Pelinkovac, schnapps, bitters…a merciful simplicity, rare in a world bombarded with information and innovation.

Baba was surprised, (and pleased), that none of those war profiteers had cast an eye on the Komiža, hadn't turned it into something with a sign above the door reading, RISTORANTE DELL'ARTE GRANDIOSA, for example, where they served those complicated foods and drinks whose names got your tongue all tangled up, like you were hammered.

For some stupid reason, Baba thought as he signaled to the barmaid to pour him another one, *people are convinced that when they enter a grandioso, whatever, that they themselves assume some kind of magical aura. That after eating some Wop or Kraut concoction with a complicated name, they're going be automatically propelled into some parallel, and infinitely superior, world. As though the place were serving side dishes of peyote or magic mushrooms, hash brownies. What the fuck is that?* Baba asked himself. *Why are we so determined to be something we'll never be, even in our wildest dreams? Why are we continually screwing each other over? "True, my salary sucks and I'm up to my ears in debts I'll be paying off till I die, but I drive an A-class car and I hang out at the Grandioso. And you? What do you drive, where do you hang out?"* If that's the way things are, he thought as he watched the foam spill over the edge of the mug and across the barmaid's beefy fingers, *then the only thing left for me to do in this evolutionary struggle is to root for the cockroach. They're okay; they mind their own business and don't act like assholes.*

The barmaid brought Baba a fresh mug of beer. He wondered whether the woman would now change into a cloud of butterflies, whether one would flutter down onto a rose, which Baba would pluck, and then all the doors would open up to him, the real doors, the ones everyone wants access to, because behind these doors, there are no disconnected phones, no overdrawn notices from the bank, no crowds in the tram, no chalk outlines of bodies on the sidewalk...

No way, Baba shook his head. The Komiža was a time warp in which nothing happened. Time had stopped in here a long time ago. Baba often thought of himself as an entity stuck in time. You can't start all over at the age of forty-six. All you can do is wait. And waiting's a lot more enjoyable with a beer to keep you company, right?

Baba chugged his beer, put his money on the counter, and went out into the street. Into a world where people are collapsing on the sidewalk, hanging on to life by the skin of their teeth, and rushing around, totally clueless that sooner or later they're going to be traveling along a street with no exit.

2. High Tea and the International Laureate

Robi locked the door to the bookstore after the girl came in. She'd been getting on his last nerve for twelve minutes already (twelve minutes after closing time, by the way) browsing through the books on the shelves. It was another lackluster day during which he'd sold maybe five or six books, mostly those psycho-manuals, self-help and so on. They were selling like hotcakes these days.

You've got no money to go on vacation, and the days are insanely long. What are you going to do with so much time? Out of sheer boredom, you start dealing with yourself, which of course drives you insane. There's nothing worse than dealing with yourself. It's depressing; it bums you out. You try to extricate yourself from this mindset. You play cards in the park, stare into the void, do crossword puzzles, read various expert advice in the newspapers and those manuals. And when nothing helps, you jump off a high-rise. I guarantee that will help you liberate yourself from yourself.

There's a nutcase who comes into the bookstore regularly, reporting the latest suicides to Robi. Half the city knows him, he's always been a nutcase, always circling around the downtown area, hassling people with his stories. But ever since an icicle slid off a roof last winter and hit him on the head, he's really been out there. Since then he's focused specifically on suicides. More work than you can handle, every day a jumper, someone shooting himself and so on.

He had popped into the bookstore again that night. That is, stood in the doorway and declared morosely, "Nothing."

And Robi said, "What are you gonna do? Tomorrow'll be better." And the guy left, shaking his head in confusion. And then the girl came in.

Robi knew right away she wasn't going to buy anything. She didn't have the look of a book buyer, no addictive gleam in the eye, and had probably come in just to kill time before meeting a boyfriend or someone. She didn't even look at him when she came in, just circled the shelves, touching the bindings with her fingers. He stood at a respectful distance, watching her. Jet-black hair, white sleeveless T-shirt, playing a solo on the book covers with those long fingers (God, the things she could do with those fingers!), an aristocratic, kingly ass (like that King's tea), a tight denim skirt. *Turn around*, Robi commands her, *turn around and look at me. Drown me in an endless flood of pure sex unadulterated by love.* But she didn't turn around, gave no sign that she was even aware of his presence.

Just kept stroking those bindings with the tips of her fingers.

Or she'd take a book, sort of weigh it in her hand, and put it back on the shelf.

She didn't even blink when Robi switched off the lights in the bookstore. Didn't get the message, so the only thing left for him to do was count the seconds and minutes, and you know how time slows down in situations like this. And then the girl launched herself toward the exit, no thank you, no goodbye, and Robi, with a look of relief on his face—the kind you get when you've been holding your piss for an eternity and finally make it to a bathroom—turned the key in the lock.

He stood for a while in the shadows staring into nothingness. People were gliding down the street, the lights of the display window illuminating them, the dresses clinging to women's hips. The windows of the Komiža gleamed ice-blue. And then Robi noticed something that took him even farther back into the shadows. Baba came out of the Komiža. He stood there looking uncertainly to the left, then the right, trying to figure out which direction to take.

Watching him, Robi reluctantly recalled times past. And a different Baba. Baba the writer (even though he'd only written one book, Robi told himself). Baba, the guy everyone was talking about, they had high expectations for him, but he never hid the fact that he didn't give a flying fuck about writing. "It's a rotten job, like working in the salt mines," he said, "and I don't work while I drink." And it was a fact; he'd just ooze into the skin of his characters and get bombed. Why did Baba do this? Those are the kind of things we'll never understand; they're the reasons people end up in prison with fifteen-year murder bids, or begging in front of the cathedral, or sitting in a government office controlling the heroin trade. The years passed by, and Baba was more or less forgotten, like all those other five-minute wonders.

It needs to be said right away that Robi couldn't stand Baba. He couldn't stand him in that specific way writers couldn't stand other writers. In other words, he couldn't tolerate him in a "collegial" way. Here's the way things stood—Robi wrote poems. He'd even published a few collections, which had gone unnoticed, for the most part, by critics and public alike. And for some reason, he held Baba responsible. Believed his books would have done better, even very well, if it hadn't been for Baba's fucking book. Felt that Baba had attracted the attention of the public away from his elegant poetry by his use of cheap street anecdotes and other trickery. Sometimes it had even made Robi nauseous. He was known for his sniveling and rages against moronic critics that, because of Baba, hadn't recognized his genius. During those times, Robi would fantasize the following situation:

So, he had found foreign publishers for the book of poems that the half-witted local critics had ignored, and it had won a prestigious international award. The local media, which had thus far cruelly ignored him, now lined up begging for interviews, but he rejected them all with cold contempt, one by one, agreeing only to speak for television, prime time, of course, right after the evening news. The interview is sheer perfection; Robi comes out looking like a genius, and then succeeds in making fools out of the entire cultural elite. And then comes the part that gives Robi a major boner—afterward Robi goes over to the Quasar Café, out in front, and there's complete silence, silence, silence, everyone fucking fixated on the international laureate, looking at him and not knowing how to act in such a situation, because here's Robi in his supernatural version, this is a big deal, he's come over right from TV, hasn't forgotten the old gang, and then check this out, two girls Baba'd been boring to death with his primitive moves just moments earlier, these two beauties start to clap, first quietly, and then louder and louder, and then the whole crowd in front of the café joins in, they're all fucking clapping for Robi, standing ovations, man, and the two beauties run over toward Robi and throw themselves into his arms, weeping with joy, and Robi hugs them, takes them over to the bar, and orders them drinks, orders everyone drinks, everyone except Baba, who's standing at the side like a stepchild, just like he's standing now in front of the Komiža, looking left, right, with no clue where he's going.

What's his fricking problem? Robi's thinking as he watches him. *Pissed off because someone didn't show up for a meeting, or he's lost, or just setting his course?*

And then he realized Baba was just looking for someone to have that last drink with him. Chances were he wouldn't find anyone he knew these days. His generation had settled down, been off the streets for ages already. Nobody was in the Quasar, Blato, or Diana bars. Nobody was late for a meeting with Baba, he was just hoping desperately to see someone, anyone, he could have one last drink with before going home.

Robi held his breath as Baba looked toward the bookstore. He stared for a long time into the display window, and then, hunched over and weaving, made his way down Masarykova Street.

At the same moment, the book fondler appeared in front of the display window with some guy. They stopped and started discussing something. It seemed to be serious. He did most of the talking, and then she would shake her head no and slide away from his grasp like a cobra whenever he'd reach his hand out to her. But it didn't look like she was afraid of him.

What a pussy, Robi thought as the guy started getting more heated up. *Can't handle defeat like a gentleman, that's your problem. And you're finished, finito, the end, you can see that from an airplane. Sooner or later you meet up with your other half, it's not unusual, it happens to a lot of people, it happened to your girl, she came in here awhile ago, recognized in me her long lost other half, the one she dreams about at night, and is letting me know now, by dumping you right in front of the book store. Nothing can help you now—threats, blackmail, begging—nothing.*

These were the thoughts swirling around in Robi's head as he watched the slinky cobra dance. And then things got really ugly. The guy hit the girl in the face. Horrified, her eyes skittered around like loose bullets and fixed on a spot somewhere in the sky. Robi rushed to the door, unlocked it, and leapt out onto the sidewalk.

The guy didn't back down, assumed one of those kung-fu movie stances, and looked Robi right in the eye.

And the girl looked at Robi.

And the passersby looked at Robi.

Robi felt like he was in front of a firing squad.

"Just a second," he mumbled, and disappeared into the bookstore.

He returned with a machete in one hand and a roll of toilet paper in the other, both of which had been hanging on the wall of the bookstore along with a woven metal pipe and a military helmet as part of an artistic installation. He stood there with a stunned look on his face, holding those two things in his hands, and then something unbelievable happened—force capitulated to art.

"Listen," said the guy, putting down his hands, "I don't want trouble."

Robi, in a daze, continued to stare at him.

"Okay, everything's cool," the guy said, turned around, and left.

Robi watched him go. Then looked down at the machete and toilet paper. They looked so ridiculous in his hands. And then his eyes searched for the girl. But she was nowhere to be seen.

3. A musical lighter and gypsy dogs

A Muzak version of the *Love Story* theme song rose up above the chattering-mumbling-giggling-chewing-sipping-buzzing that exemplified the front of the Utrina marketplace.

"Is that your lighter or someone's cell phone?" Baba asked.

"Someone's cell phone," Kančeli said angrily. "My lighter doesn't play shit."

Yeah, right. Kančeli's managed to find one that plays "Für Elise." Baba hasn't managed to find a lighter similar to his, he's just run into Kančeli coming back from downtown, and now he starts telling him about how he got kicked out of Istria the other day.

"For loitering," Baba says. "All I did was go to Marlera to see if there was a view of Galiola from there."

"Marlera, Galiola?" says Kančeli while fiddling with his stubby lighter, which had a picture of a dolphin jumping out of the sea foam on its side, and a silver firing mechanism, also in the shape of a dolphin.

"Marlera is a cape, and Galiola is a cliff Šoljan and Angel's ship crashes into and sinks. You know, in that book *Other People on the Moon*," he adds.

"Okay," says Kančeli.

"And then the cops jack me up in front of a shop in Šišan."

"Where's Šišan?" Kančeli asks.

"Šišan?" Baba raises his eyebrows. "Well, it's right across from Omaruru, you just head north on the fourteenth meridian."

"Aha," says Kančeli.

"Good day, good day, your ID please, where are you staying, no-where, where are you heading, none of your business, what did you say, what do you want from me... In short, I was not looking to get into a hassle there with them, but they definitely had a hard-on for me. You know, when some nancy-ass tries to play the big shot. For no reason. They didn't know what to charge me with. I didn't do anything wrong, they just wanted to bust me. So they pulled out the loitering routine from somewhere and ordered me out of Istria."

"Give me a break," said Kančeli.

"Seriously. They escorted me in their car all the way to the tunnel and said if they ever caught me loitering again..."

"Well, fuck me," Kančeli sputtered. "A man isn't even free to walk around anymore. They're telling you where to go, when, how...like they're charging you for the spot you're standing on, the air you breathe."

He became silent, irritated, breathing in the odor of gas-perme-ated air and freshly mown grass. Baba regarded him with interest, as though sitting before him he had some demented Martian spending his first day on Earth.

Kančeli wasn't too far off that characterization. Imagine a guy who simply rejected electricity, the phone, the TV, computers, and so on, when today, almost every little contraption emits its own source of ra-diation. A guy who says, what do I need it for? I don't need it. I just get a headache from all those things, all the pictures, sounds, and informa-tion. Fuck that, I don't want to spend my life working at something that screws with my head. Can you imagine a guy like that?

That's Kančeli. Lives in a cave on the ninth floor of a high-rise that smells like wax, petroleum, and paraffin; works in a carwash in the neighborhood, when he feels like it, as much as he needs to, and does a little painting and so on. Kančeli, who's now pulling out a cigarette and lighting up.

"Nannannnananana," says the lighter.

"Pretty cool, huh?" says Kančeli, looking at his lighter.

Baba shrugged his shoulders, finding it far from cool.

"Really," says Kančeli, "why'd you go to Istria?"

"Oh, you know," Baba says, "Vera was in a bad mood, so I just went out, got in the car—the street was calling out to me."

"I get it," says Kančeli.

"But what's the deal with that asshole Robi?" says Baba.

"What about him?"

"I'm in town, standing in front of the Komiža," Baba says, "and the whole time I have this feeling someone's watching me from the bookstore. I'll bet that asshole was inside, watching me in the dark."

"Aw, forget it," says Kančeli. "What I don't understand is how we can bring ourselves to spend our money here."

"What do you mean?" says Baba.

"What do I mean?" says Kančeli. "You know the owner here's a Muzzie from Kosovo. That's what I mean."

"So what?" says Baba.

"Well, shit," says Kančeli, losing patience, "don't you know how gypsies are treated in Albania?"

"So what do gypsies and Albania have to do with this café?" says Baba, surprised.

Kančeli, not hearing Baba's question-reaction routine, says, "Well, don't you know that gypsies are pretty much treated like dogs in Albania?"

"How do you know that?" says Baba, amazed.

"I met a gypsy from Albania, and he told me that."

"That gypsies are basically treated like dogs in Albania?"

"Yeah."

"If I were to give it a little thought, I'd say that was okay," says Baba.

"What do you mean, okay?" says Kančeli, astonished.

"Easy," says Baba. "Did your new friend happen to tell you how gypsies treat dogs?"

"No, he didn't tell me that," Kančeli answered, confused.

"There you go," says Baba. "If you really wanted the truth, you'd ask him that, and he'd tell you how dogs do pretty well with the gypsies. Better than the women. The cats have it the worst. Cats are fucked. They're down on the bottom, you know. And then come the women, and then the dogs."

"Oh, fuck," he says, looking at his watch, "I've got to go." He put a rumpled ten-kuna bill down on the table and left, not waiting for Kančeli's thoughts on the issue of the women, dogs, and cats.

And Kančeli remained, looking out into the New Zagreb night. Into the windows lit up by the flickering images on the screen, at an Irish setter nosing around a cement flowerpot, the poplars reaching up toward the strawberry sky. Staring at those black trees and the sky, which had absorbed the lights of the city, Kančeli imagined it must be the end of the world. That scene, he thought, it's a scene that belongs to the end of the world. It just wasn't possible that there could be anything at all behind those black poplars swaying in the wind.

4. A mirror that lies, the Vienna Boys' Choir, and a nun from the Order of Holy Theresa Orlowsky

Vera was sitting on the couch in the living room, staring at the Ikea shelf full of books and thinking how a glass of chardonnay would be just the thing to...

JUST THE THING TO WHAT? *This senseless evening, the party I didn't organize, the dinner I didn't cook, and Baba getting hung up outside somewhere.*

She looked through the window out into the night, as though expecting Baba to burst in from that direction. Instead of Baba, a firefly fluttered in, which she would come across the next morning dead on the floor next to the bed, or the bookshelf, under the kitchen table, or wherever it was it had decided to die.

For now, it fluttered into the kitchen, attracted by the light above the sink. Vera got up and went after it, attracted by the bottles of wine on the wine rack. She opened a bottle of chardonnay, poured some into a coffee cup and, circling around, came to a stop in front of the mirror in the hallway, a huge mirror attached to the sliding doors of the pantry that hid all those things Vera would like to get rid of, if only she could convince herself she'd never need them again.

"Cheers, black bags under the eyes," she said, raising the cup to the mirror. "It's amazing how good you look on me. Congratulations! And the wrinkles, too, I am proud of you, and I love you all. So what if I'm getting old," she declared to the mirror. "The years, my friend, are no problem at all, no catastrophe; on the contrary, they provide great protection from men, in case you didn't know. And for your information, I feel fine. I finally feel at peace; I can relax, actually feel good today about reaching the big Four-O."

She took a sip of wine and thought about how that moron Kančeli was right when he said wine tasted the same whether you drank it out of a wine glass, a coffee cup, or a plastic glass. Then she returned to the mirror.

"So should I get a face-lift or dye my hair?" she asked, aggravated. "Oh, go take a flying fuck! I'm not asking you to lie to me, and I'm not asking for expert advice, either. You know, it would drive me nuts if men started hitting on me again. You have no idea what it's like when you just want to have a quiet cup of coffee somewhere and some imbecile starts giving you the eye, and then comes over and begins talking a bunch of bullshit to you. That's how it goes, for years and years, from the time your titties start popping out until the skin on your neck starts sagging. You know how it is. So don't talk nonsense. I've finally reached the point where I am a happy woman—CONTENTED AND HAPPY!"

She made an angry gesture with her hand, returned to the living room, and lounged back on the couch. She didn't feel like wine anymore. She was mad at the mirror, the cup that had ruined the taste of the wine, the firefly that had decided to die in her apartment, at Baba, and everyone else who had forgotten it was her birthday.

Okay, true, her mother called, but that had consisted of five minutes of agony, five minutes being bombarded with the same question: *why don't you have a baby?…why don't you have a baby?…why don't you have a baby? Because I already have a baby, Mama,* she had wanted to cry out. She treated Baba as though he were a retarded child. *And how do you expect me to have a baby with a child,* she wanted to say, but instead of that she answered automatically, *I'm too old for that, Mama…I'm too old for that, Mama…I'm too old for that, Mama…*

She got a card from Duda.

"Have so many years gone by already? When Diddley was doing 'Bo's a Lumberjack,' and Chuck and Jerry were shaking it up, *A Clockwork Orange* was out, Burroughs' *TTTE* and Bukowski's 'Run with the Hunted', Leary was messing around with the sacred mushrooms, Laing was doing his evil thing, Hooker and Waters wailing their blues…and you were CRYING your first blues…wow, those were the years!"

WOW, what a load of shit, Vera thought as she read the message.

Where did she come up with this stuff? What was she talking about? Rock bit the dust a long time ago. And all those people, too, I guess. Or they soon would. What is this, a birthday card or a catalog? Crying the blues? Give me a break. What time-space was this woman living in? It's like she moved to Podunk, Iowa, instead of London.

This is what Vera was thinking as she read the card from Duda, an old friend she used to drink coffee with at least twice a week until she had moved to London. They met during school entrance exams, and the friendship had lasted and lasted and lasted, like the taste of that chewing gum from the TV commercials. And even when the taste was gone, they went on seeing each other, meeting up in town; the chewing habit kept their friendship in good shape.

"Those were really okay times," was what Vera would say if some magazine pollster were to call her up and ask her about the period when she had met Duda. "A little studying here, a little partying there, a lot of nights spent at the Zvečka, Blato, and Quasar. And yeah, a lot of sex. A huge amount of sex. Nobody made a big thing out of a simple fuck, at least not in the company I kept."

Tom didn't make a big thing out of it, either. Tom, the blonde

English Lit student, whose face made a regular appearance in the dreams of a lot of girls on the Zvečka-Quasar night circuit. They met one night at the Quasar, and five minutes later, a cop busted them half-naked on a bench in the woods below Krleža's house. "Get out of here; do you know whose house this is?" Not even the cop had had a problem with it. Communism had sort of lightened up during that time, at least on the issue of sex, but the cop still couldn't allow the gardens of the Croatian classic to be desecrated. "Tuškanac is a big park, go find a place there." But they could only hold out until they reached the old open-air movie theater. Yeah, yeah, the lust was overpowering, almost painful. Tom lived way out in the Trnsko district, Vera with her parents, and they couldn't wait for a better opportunity. They got right down to business. That morning, hair covered with leaves, clothes grubby, they headed down toward Ilica Street, and Tom initiated a conversation about living together. Said he couldn't imagine living with someone. "Why? Because I'm too hyper," he said, "I can't ever just stop and think about making a move, I go with the flow, go with the flow."

Meanwhile, Tom had waded in Vera's pond for two whole years. Remaining loyal to the fluvial theory he had developed that summer morning, Tom later took off for Canada. Did he remember Vera's birthday? Maybe. Maybe at this very moment—and over there it would be early afternoon—he was telling some bartender as he gestured for another beer, "You know what, buddy, your problem is you think too much. That's why you'll never make it out of here; you'll never meet Vera." "Who in the hell is Vera?" asks the bartender. "Today's Vera's birthday," says Tom, raising his beer mug.

Why was Vera thinking about Tom? He'd left less behind than anyone else had. A few pictures they took together, those insipid odds and ends people give to one another when they're in love. And his Conrad squeezed in between Susan Sontag and Bukowski on the bookshelf. *Styles of Radical Will. Erections, Ejaculations, Exhibitions, and General Tales of Ordinary Madness.* Vera gets up, takes *Heart of Darkness* from the shelf, and starts to read. Reads until she hears the sound of a key in the door. This sound ripped Vera away from the breathtaking landscape through which Kurtz was passing; she was suddenly gripped with anxiety. She put away the book and looked tensely toward the door. The trick was in the key. The sound of a key in the lock—which would otherwise eliminate various forms of anxiety, especially when loved ones were out and about—this same sound has a devastating effect on Vera. At the sound of a key in the lock, Vera freezes up like the screen of a virus-infected computer. Actually, Vera thinks of Baba as a virus programmed to destroy her life. "You've fucked up all my systems," she often tells him. When Baba's out somewhere, things still make sense somehow. Vera reads, dusts the shelves *(you'd think I live in the middle of a fucking dust storm)*, writes down notes for an essay on literary theory she was supposed to have submitted long ago to a publisher, surfs the Net...She relaxes, you know, forgets where she is, just floats out somewhere, using the same devices we all use. And then, pow! That key in the lock. And her heart skips a beat and then stops.

"What are you reading?" Baba asks from the door.

Vera was evaluating him. She didn't hear that rumbling quality in his voice. It seemed he was walking okay. Wasn't swaying or reaching for support from the wall. And he was looking her straight in the eye. Had that chardonnay dulled Vera's sense of smell? There were only a few inches left in the bottle.

"Good evening," she said, "Happy Birthday, blah blah blah."

"Another one?" Baba said. "How fast the years go by."

Vera watched him as he approached the bookshelf, searching for a gap between the books.

"Reading *Heart of Darkness*, huh?" Baba said.

Baba was great with books. Much better than with people.

"Amazing how many worthless talents you have," Vera said. "Where have you been?"

"With Kančeli."

"That potted plant?" she smiled disdainfully.

"Just because he's not a CEO and doesn't drive a BMW doesn't make him a potted plant," said Baba dryly.

"Listen, I don't want to discuss Kančeli or anyone like him," she said.

"You started it," Baba said, kneeling before her. "Happy Birthday!" And then kissed her.

"You've been drinking again," said Vera, wrinkling her nose.

She detected the sweet smell of beer, but not hard liquor.

"A little," Baba said.

"A LITTLE? How much is that in the Croatian language?" Vera asked.

Figuring it out in fingers, Baba stopped at seven.

"Fuck it, Baba," she said, "it's not fair."

"Everything's under control," he said. "Listen, what's the plan for tonight?"

Vera considered whether it was wiser to get into it with Baba or go along with his little game.

"Well, let's just say that if the mailman, the electrician, or the chimney sweep rang the bell right now, I'd drag them into bed with me immediately. But if it's you we're talking about, then no way without an appropriate gift."

Baba stood up, unzipped his pants, took out his dick, and smiled like one of those Vienna Choir boys. "Is this appropriate, ma'am?"

"You're a moron, Baba," she said, checking out the white silk bow tied around its base, "you're a real moron."

Baba extended his arms, smiling like the entire Choir.

"Okay," Vera decided, "just this one time, but I swear, Baba..."

Later that night, listening to Baba's slow breathing, Vera gazed out into the illuminated windows of the buildings outside, wondering what the people who lived there were doing. The scenes she imagined were entirely ordinary. Someone was watching television and reaching with one hand for some lemon-flavored jellybeans. Another was turning the pages of a book, another pouring beer into a glass. Some were fighting about which TV program to watch, some were carrying on a hot discussion about government policies. Some were looking at old photo albums and laughing as they connected the photos with the events. And some were just screwing.

The scene developing behind the window next to Kančeli's cave on the ninth floor wasn't included in the top ten Vera had imagined before falling asleep. Behind that window, Stjepan (if he had a visiting card it would read, in fancy letters, RETIRED SAILOR AND CONSTRUC-TION WORKER), his lips clenched and arms extended, the palms facing downward, was twirling around on his axis. A cat with sleek black fur, a powerful body, and a banged-up head was sitting on the window sill, watching with undisguised interest as the tough old man in short pants whirled around like a top, and thinking how entertaining it all was.

Stjepan had naturally never heard of the Furies, ghost stars, or the divine movements of the dervishes, but he was nonetheless perform-ing some kind of dervish dance.

Ever since he'd found that brochure last week about the rituals of Tibetan monks, Stjepan's life in retirement had risen to a new level. Stjepan had considered the crumpled up brochure, covered with oil and coffee spots, a gift from Fate. And Fate had rarely been generous with him. Once he won a small lotto payout (half the players won the same thing), a six-pack in a New Year's raffle in 1960-something. And a few years ago at the tram station, he'd found a scrofulous black cat that had since assumed the identity of Čombe, a beast that terrified all the cats and most of the dogs in the neighborhood. Stjepan had never found money on the sidewalk, never sat down at a table where someone had left behind a lighter or a pack of cigarettes, though he himself had left behind a ton of lighters and what not. Stjepan never bothered about things like that. He was a practical man. He didn't dwell on what had already happened. *It's the past*, he'd think, *something that can't be changed, and only fools waste their time on things they can't change.* Stjepan just forged ahead, minus the extra baggage.

He'd spent his life on the decks of freighters and construction sites between Munich and Frankfurt. He wasn't religious, and didn't believe in laws, politics, love, or, especially, marriage. He thought it was stupid for sailors to get married (any idiot could get married and then just sail away), and later, even when he started working in construction, he continued to hold that opinion. People like Stjepan were rarely given anything. People like him had to struggle to get a smile out of a prostitute, and that's why Stjepan interpreted the brochure lying at his feet on the sidewalk as a SIGN. What kind of sign he didn't yet know, but it was worth a try.

He read through the brochure, studied the drawings of the various movements, and was now performing the first ritual, spinning around in place until a mild dizziness warned him that searching for youthful vibes was okay as long as you didn't get too carried away. Stjepan really wasn't expecting any miracle. Miracles happened to other people; he just read about them in newspapers, the Old Testament, and the like. He didn't believe that by performing these movements he'd be thrust back into his youth, as he'd recently been thrust into his seventies, that wasn't really important to him. *Big deal, youth*. He wouldn't want to go through it again.

He looked at youth the same way he did those really, really tight jeans. *Something that you don't feel comfortable in*, he thought as he did the Tibetan version of the belly dance, *something that squeezes you, that gives The Boss, bulging as is his nature, blisters, something you can hardly wait to get rid of, be liberated from, you and The Boss.*

"We've still got a lot of battles to fight, don't we, General," he says out loud, not to himself or the cat. Feels his partner in conversation coming to life, swelling, so he rushes to the phone, calls, says, "Hi, it's Štef, come over."

And a woman's voice from the other end says, "I can't, I'm stuck babysitting my granddaughter."

And Stjepan says, "What am I going to do now?"

And the woman's voice says, "I don't know."

And Stjepan says, "Jesus."

And the woman's voice doesn't say anything. And Stjepan hangs up the phone, puts in a video, and then the body of a nun from the Order of Saint Theresa Orlowsky radiates out from the screen.

"What are you looking at," Stjepan says to the cat. "It's easy for you; you can lick yourself."

5. The copper bee and people with eyes like eels

Vera sits blinking at the computer with her legs tucked underneath her, satisfied with the results she's gotten from a quick Google browse in the wide-open range of the Internet. Tom Kola isn't unknown out there, at least where the first name is entered as separate from the last. And where Tom and Kola came up together, a web site for some marketing agency was given.

Waiting for the page to come up, Vera noticed how dry her lips were. She could hardly manage to swallow the air bubble in her throat, and her heart was beating more quickly. *Come on*, she thought, *what are you doing? Like I'm a fucking groupie or something trying to get a movie star's autograph. Like I'm bursting in on Tom begging him for something. Money, lunch—or informing him that he's the father of the child I gave birth to after he took off for Canada and to please take note of that. Brrrr*, Vera shivered at the thought of that combination.

She found on the page a text about post-Warhol candy boxes, or something like that, signed by Tom Kola. She read a few sentences and cried out. *There aren't very many people in the world who can pontificate like that*, she thought, and sent a short message to the address.

> **Hey, Tom Kola,**
> **Well, I'm sitting here thinking about whether the**
> **world is lucky enough to have two (or more) of you.**
> **If there are, and if you're the original—and that thing**
> **about Warhol and the baklava tells me you are—then**
> **hey, check in. You know, so I don't waste time here with**
> **that other T.K. I don't even know. Greetings from Vera**

And Kančeli was lying on the mattress listening to the trams rattling down Dubrovnik Avenue. After a few minutes of that, he got up, did a few squats and pushups, put coffee on the camp stove, took a spoonful of honey, and watched the cars creeping around the marketplace.

"Hey, Čombe, hi," he said, seeing the huge, black head peeking through the marijuana plants in the flowerpot below the window. "Out for a morning stroll, huh? Stay away from those plants, my friend; don't even think about eating those. Is the old guy still sleeping? Did he get laid last night? Want a cracker? You don't. A little honey? Don't want that, either. Sorry, I don't have anything else. I can get you some fish later. By the way, is it true that cats don't even like fish, and that they eat it only when they're desperate? And you're not desperate, are you, friend?"

Kančeli drank the coffee out of a tin cup decorated with smiling cows. Every morning he drank coffee from this cup, and only rarely did he recall that it had belonged to his daughter Maja. That was a long time ago.

Maja was with her mother in Pula now. *And SHE had hooked up with some cop*, Kančeli thought disgustedly, *maybe one of those that kicked Baba out of Istria.*

"You'll never make anything out of yourself," his wife had told him once, not even bothering to disguise her loathing and distaste.

That evening, like so many others, Kančeli had come home dead drunk, swaying to the rhythm of the sidewalk, the whiskey, and the beer. Maja started crying when she saw him. He sat her down in his lap and shoved a box into her hand. "Look what I brought you," he said. Maja opened the box and pulled out a copper bee. Held it in her hand, sniffling.

"Just you cry," he told her, "tomorrow morning your tears are going to turn into bees." Her tears didn't turn into bees the next morning. No miracle at all took place that morning. They just packed up their things and went to Pula. Many years had passed since then.

And this morning Kančeli was thinking about Maja and her mother, without regret or sorrow, the way he thought about a lot of other lost opportunities. He knew mistakes could be corrected, but not today. Today was a bad day for correcting mistakes.

He washed out the cup and got dressed while looking out the window. Tomorrow, too, he would watch the cars circling the marketplace, go have coffee with the boys, then home, a nap in the afternoon, the cafeteria in the evening—no miracles were going to happen tomorrow, either. *Aw, fuck it, this wasn't a time for miracles*, he concluded as he left for the marketplace.

Kančeli helped a shopkeeper unload crates of fish. When buyers requested it, he'd clean the fish. On a good day, he could earn fifty kuna. More on Fridays. Today was a bad day. He only had five, six kuna rattling around in his pocket. He smoked as he considered the frozen, empty eyes of the mullet, hake, catfish, and eel. He noticed that a lot of the people had the same empty, frozen eyes. "See you later," he told the shopkeeper, and went over to the cafeteria.

Žac, Beli, Jajo, the whole gang from the neighborhood was there. The waitress put some draft beer down in front of him. Kančeli asked her if she'd marry him. She said no problem, as soon as she finished her shift.

"Don't you get sick of that fish stench?" Jajo asked him.

Kančeli shrugged his shoulders. "You gotta do something," he said.

"Check this out," Žac said.

A girl in an indigo blue dress was coming down the sidewalk. They watched her until she got all the way to the supermarket.

"Fuckin' A!" Beli said.

"Yes indeed!" said Jajo.

Kančeli drank up his beer and put some change on the counter.

"Jajo will give you the rest," he told the waitress.

"Aren't you going to have another one?" Jajo asked.

Kančeli waved him off and left. He watched the kids in the schoolyard play soccer for a while. Then he went home, took a box of crackers from the kitchen shelf, and, as he chewed, read down the list of hospitals taped to the sliding doors.

Marked with a fluorescent pen was the Center for the Prevention of Addiction, Red Cross, Friendship Park, Jarun. This yellowed clipping from the newspaper reminded Kančeli of his wife. It was her discharge letter.

6. How Vera almost cut off her finger and how Baba couldn't remember what an ashtray was called

Statistics are the God of numbers, a diabolical web that holds an entire army of poor people hostage, the official drug of the entire world. They are the poetry of federal bureaucrats, illustrating to them that a prisoner with a death sentence doesn't really have it all that bad, that there are many, many good years ahead of him.

This is how it's done. The past year, Baba was out of commission for 202 days, 15 percent more than the year before. Of those 202 days, five were for a really rotten Asian flu, six for a virus, thirteen for allergies, eighty-eight for being in a bad mood for a variety of reasons, and the rest, a full ninety days, for varying states of drunkenness or hangover. The first six months of this year, Baba'd been more or less out of commission for 144 days already. Five days virus, two weeks allergies, forty-five days bad mood caused by various aspects of daily existence, twelve days in a state of euphoria listening to old records and smoking all day and all night because the record player had finally been repaired, and the crowning touch: sixty-eight days drunk or hungover.

Vera had no reason to doubt the stark numbers, the merciless mathematical logic that declared Baba had set a new record. She informed Baba.

"You've sunk to that," he said bitterly. "You've been taking notes, like a spy, of my illnesses, my drunks and hangovers?"

"Of course not, sweetheart," said Vera. "I'm not taking notes on all your stupidities, only on the days I've lost. I've got a right to do that, don't I?"

Actually, it was one of the nicer mornings. The dining room smelled of coffee and fresh bread. Radio 101 was belting out some bad reggae, stray cats were coming out of cracks in the walls of neighboring buildings, stretching out in the sun, looking at the dogs sideways, kids were having a heated argument about some foul, was it out of bounds or not, Baba was rolling himself a cigarette, swaying to the rhythm of the music, saying he was sorry he had to be in bed, and Vera saying, "fuck one morning, some people waste their entire lives" and Baba saying "what do you mean?" and Vera pulling out the statistics.

"Fine," said Baba. "Can you tell me what I've done wrong lately to piss you off so much?"

"Well, it would take quite awhile for me to list all your past screw-ups," Vera said. "But, if you insist, here are a few examples of what an asshole you are. For instance, last year I went alone to have my fucking abortion and came home from the hospital alone because you were drinking somewhere, and because you basically didn't give a shit."

Baba looked out the window. A sparrow was perched on the satellite antenna, taking a crap, but Baba didn't see that. He was thinking about how cruel and serious Vera had become. Like she'd succumbed to the mathematician's syndrome in *The Little Prince* and forgotten how to play.

"And then," Vera continued, "when I almost cut off my finger with that knife. I called you at work and asked you to come and take me to the hospital, but you didn't come because you managed to get hung up, by the way, drinking beer with someone."

"I came," Baba said.

"I waited two hours for you, Baba," said Vera, "a full two hours, and then I took a taxi to get my finger stitched up. And as they were sewing up my finger, I just felt so terribly sorry that I wasn't able to wait at home for you to take me to the hospital."

"It's not fair to rub my nose in that now," Baba said.

"Oh, yeah?" Vera said. "And you running around all the time, coming home just to sleep and lick your wounds, you call that fair? But that's not the worst thing with you."

"Stop," Baba said. "Before you continue, I'd like to inform you that I have no connections whatsoever to pedophilia, child porn on the Internet, or anything remotely similar."

It was a pitiful attempt, and Baba knew it. Vera just waved him off and gave him a pale, sickly smile.

"The worst thing with you is that you've given up. Actually, you gave up quite awhile ago; now you're just hanging on."

Maybe, Baba thought, *but you betrayed everything you used to be.*

"You don't write, you don't read, you don't care about anything, you don't even watch soccer anymore, you—just—drink—and—hang on. And I can't deal with you anymore; I can't even look at you."

Baba stared at the blue glass ashtray trying to remember what the object was called.

"When you're not in a bad mood, you're drinking. When you're not drunk, you're hungover. When you're not hungover, you're in a bad mood."

"Not true," Baba said without an iota of defensive zeal. And still couldn't remember what an ashtray was called.

"Come on, get serious, Baba. People who've known each other, lived together for so long, shouldn't be talking like this to each other. Things are substantially fucked up, and it'd be better to call it quits before we fuck everything up completely."

"And that means?" said Baba, staring at the ashtray.

"That means you need to leave, Baba."

"Leave?"

"Yeah, Baba, pack your things and go."

"Ashtray," Baba said as it dawned on him. "This is a fucking ashtray."

7. Why Robi is nauseated by the X Generation

Robi had been thinking lately about how he had almost gotten involved in a fistfight. He couldn't figure out what had induced him to confront that guy. The waters of violence were waters he never swam in. What sense did it make getting involved in something that had nothing to do with him? And what would have happened if the dude had pulled out a gun? That could easily have happened, Robi thought. People are more likely these days to have guns under their jackets than a Discman. I would've pissed my pants and fainted, if the guy didn't shoot me first, Robi concluded bitterly. And because of what? Some girl who didn't even thank him afterward. And what's more, she took off right in the middle of everything, the ungrateful cow. He exhaled, annoyed, and began to organize books on the shelves. Mind your own business, man, he told himself. The city is full of buffed-up gorillas; all you need is to piss off one of those morons, and he'd kick your ass on general principles. What am I talking about? Gorillas are okay in comparison; with them you can at least come to some kind of understanding, but with those rednecks, no way...

"Hi, remember me?"

Robi turned toward the door and there was that jet-black hair. *Oh, fuck*, he thought anxiously, *here comes trouble. What if that kung fu guy and his friends are right behind her?* He'd be screwed. They had him trapped like a rat. He had nowhere to go. He might as well sit down and cry. His rotten luck.

"Hi," she said.

But she was alone; the guy wasn't with her. Robi exhaled. Relief. How little it takes to make a human being happy. And Robi turned that relief into irony: "I was just thinking about you."

"That's nice."

As though nothing had happened, as though he hadn't almost died because of her.

"Can I come in?"

Robi was completely relaxed now. The guy was nowhere in sight.

"Only if you're going to buy something."

"No problem."

She checked out the new titles on the shelves while Robi studied her face, looking for traces of that blow. There weren't any. With or without them, it was a very pretty face. So pretty that Robi started drooling, sensing a wounded doe that has trustingly taken refuge in the lion's den, and the lion has noticed her, is showing her his benevolent face. *Oh yes, he would have her, why not? First he'd lick her wounds, and then go in for the kill...*

"What are people buying these days?"

"Excuse me?"

"What's selling these days?"

"Garbage, that's what."

"Some recommendation."

Robi shrugged his shoulders.

"And what kind of garbage is that?"

"Oh, usually the kind promoted in the media—"

Robi was prevented from finishing the first sentence of his favorite mini-speech on the influence of mass media on literature by the sudden invasion into the bookstore by a horde of kids. Five of them descended on the bookshelves, transforming the store into a Saturday market. Robi didn't like them bursting in like this, in packs. Even if they bought something, some sale book, it didn't make up for what they took out underneath their jackets. That's why Robi gave out a loud whistle. They quieted down and looked at him. He explained, pointing over to the alarm box, that it was broken, and then, pointing his index and middle finger to his eyes, told them in fact these eyes were THE MOST SENSITIVE SENSORS of all, and that they shouldn't take it the wrong way, but if he caught anyone ripping off a book, he would slice off the offender's hand with that thing over there, and pointed to the machete hanging on the wall.

"Got it?" Robi asked.

The kids silently exchanged looks and left the bookstore one by one.

"You're not very nice to the customers," she said.

"What customers?" Robi asked in astonishment. "You call them customers? Those little shitheads would steal my pants right off me if I let them. Being nice to customers like that leads you straight into bankruptcy."

"Okay, I'll save you from bankruptcy," she said, taking *American Psycho* from the shelf. "Is this garbage?"

"Oh, I see you're one of the X generation."

"Excuse me?" she said.

And then he began counting off disdainfully: "Synthetic drugs, synthetic literature, synthetic sex…"

"What are you so pissed off about?" Little marks of discomfort had appeared in her eyes.

"What am I pissed off about?" he said, imitating her uneasy tone. "I'm pissed off because those kinds of books make me nauseous. That's not just ordinary garbage, it's—"

"I'm leaving," she said, returning the book to the shelf.

Robi waved her off. "It doesn't matter. The enemy is outside the gates."

She stopped and looked at him. Was he just neurotic or also dangerous?

"Sorry," he said. "I shouldn't talk like that about the books. I make my living from them."

"Actually, I came to thank you for the other day," she said.

"It's okay," Robi said.

"No, it's not okay," she said. "A person can die right on the street, wild dogs can eat you, and nobody would even…" She stopped, choking back her anger.

"Hm, yeah," Robi said, amazed by the explosion of rage. "But your boyfriend…"

"He's not my boyfriend at all," she said bitterly. "He's just a jerk who thinks if he buys you a drink he can fuck you immediately thereafter."

"I didn't know," Robi said.

"And then, if he fucks you once," she continued in the same tone, "he thinks you're his permanent property."

"Yeah," Robi said.

Now he was drooling substantially. *This is fucking excellent, what luck for a BABE LIKE THIS to fall into your arms, you're going to have to fucking fight her off…*

"Suzi," she said, extending her hand.

8. Coffee in a can and wine in a carton

hey, vera,

man, we don't hear from each other for fifteen years and you start off attacking me, typical for you and your oversized female ego. if you'd called me a moron or an asshole, ok, but thinking there might be more than one of me? but i have to admit that i was mildly pleased to get your message, i can't be ecstatic about it because i'm dead and also poisoned. that's because i arrived from new york awhile ago and on the way got poisoned by that fucking coffee in a can (whoever thought up the idea of coffee in a can can go fuck himself) and so i was sick from new york until i got home (i still live in toronto). how are you? what are you doing? are you still with baba? how's he, is he even writing? i don't see his name on the internet. who's still around from the old gang? is kančeli alive? sorry, but all that comes to mind are these questions. which is good because my mind is disintegrating, everything in it's dried up except this fucking pain. so i'm going to go now and see if i can throw up, then i'll take some pills and try to sleep. see ya...i'll write in more detail when i come back to life.

write, tom

Dear Tom,

I'm shocked you're still trying to be different from everyone else. Normal people poison themselves with food, alcohol, and things like that; you end up doing it with coffee. Coffee in a can! I didn't even know that existed. I thought the lowest the human consumer could sink to was wine in a carton. See, I haven't been in New York, haven't ever drunk anything that exotic, but I still feel dead and poisoned (good expression). Probably from the humidity here or the stink from the dump over at Jakuševac, or maybe it's just my turn to feel bad. And today is Monday, and it started out dreary first thing in the morning, and nothing can be done about it.

But other than that, not bad. For years I've been working as a junior professor in the English department. That sounds great, I mean the junior part, but unfortunately, that only applies to my status and salary, not my age.

It seems like I'll be going into retirement as a junior professor. The old gang? I don't know where those people disappeared to. Duda's in London, married some okay guy there, we see each other, have coffee (the normal way, in a cup) and so on. The rest are probably here, but I don't see them much. Everyone's in their own world with their own hassles. As far as I know, very few from our generation left the country. People our age, with our skills, aren't needed on the outside. And I swear, they're not needed here either. Plus there was the war. I mean, the years went by so fast, like in a nightmare, like you were listening to records at 78 speed, if I'm allowed to even say that in the digital age. And before we knew it, we were stuck in middle age. Fuck it, this is depressing. Want me to lie a little? That would make it better. Baba and I are still together, but that's sort of a complicated issue, and I'm not sure I want to talk about that now. There comes a time when a person has to draw the line, settle accounts, and we seem to be doing this mathematical juggling now. Baba's not writing; he stopped at that one book…He did some war reporting, and that kept him afloat, and then the war ended and, how should I say this, he sort of lost it. Didn't know what to do with himself. He's working at Agramer now as an editor and says he's going to start writing short stories. We're living in a rented apartment in Utrine, etc. Oh yeah, Kančeli is here in Utrine; he and Baba hang out. Kančeli married that Irena from Pula, they had a daughter, he had a good career in an attorney's office, and then he started hitting the bottle. Typical scene from the catalog of male stupidities, right? And when Irena packed up and moved in with her people in Pula, he really went nuts. Quit his job, sold everything in the apartment (literally everything), and is living like a hermit now. It was a real circus in the beginning. He had problems with the neighbors, the police would show up every once in a while, like, this is no way to live, no electricity, telephone, and so forth, he must be into something, maybe a dealer or a terrorist or a dangerous lunatic or something, but after a while they left him alone. Okay, hope you recover soon from the coffee in a can. Write!

Greetings from Vera

9. The KO'd boxer, Billy the Kid, and the cuckoo bird busted

All the sounds in Vera and Baba's apartment had died, one by one. No more morning radio program, no sound of vegetables being chopped, no pans clanking. There was no more bickering over recipes for fish kebabs and what cheese went best with risotto and shellfish. Miles Davis and the Gypsies had played out their trumpets. The Saturday concerts and orchestras that went with the vacuuming were cancelled. (Baba claimed the best music to vacuum by was the "Radetzky March.")

The water boiler wasn't as noisy as it used to be, and the pipes stopped dripping. All you could hear from their apartment was suppressed human hissing and the spooky sound of the television. Like that guy said: "Love lasts eternally—until marriage." Then it loses its color, smell, and taste, and metamorphoses into a series of situations like this one:

One evening Baba came into the apartment and asked what there was to eat. Vera didn't need to look at him to figure out his condition—he radiated drunkenness with the energy of a sonic boom. Crazy birds squawked and beat their wings against Vera's birdcage head when Baba came home like this. Like now. She got up and marched off to the kitchen. "Look," she said, pointing at the refrigerator. "That's a refrigerator. And that thing with the four circular tiles on top? That's an oven. The stuff on the shelf in boxes and containers, those are spices. On the shelf below, as you see, there are potatoes and pasta. Relatively quickly, a person of average intelligence can combine the contents of the refrigerator and shelves, and with the help of this appliance," she said, pointing to the oven, "prepare himself a very decent, edible meal. To start out, I'd recommend scrambled eggs."

"What the fuck's your problem?" Baba said. "I know how to cook; I cook better than you do."

Baba still hadn't gotten it. This outburst of rage caught him unprepared. He stood in the middle of the kitchen, staring in astonishment at a decorative wall tile painted with teapots and lemons. What he had just experienced, he thought, was either based on some tragic misunderstanding, or the result of some event about which he knew nothing and therefore couldn't know how to respond, or (and this possibility Baba considered most likely) it was the consequence of some horrible trauma from Vera's childhood he had failed to pick up on earlier.

"Okay," he said, "what's your problem?"

"What's my problem?"

"Yeah."

"You. You're my problem."

"Me, why?" Baba said, surprised.

Vera hated what she was about to say. The answer she'd be using was one she'd heard a hundred times in movies, but she never could have imagined herself saying those words. For a lot of things, new words haven't been discovered, and the old ones are so corny that you don't know what to do with them. So, should you say them and open yourself up to the risk you'll come out sounding like a moron, or should you just keep your trap shut? This is what Vera was confronted with now, a totally ridiculous situation, but she didn't have much of a choice, she was forced into saying these words, Baba had forced her to speak them, and she hated Baba for it, she hated herself, hated, hated, hated…

"Because you're a drunk, Baba," she hissed, "because you're a boozer, because alcohol is eating you up. Look at yourself," she said, and ran into the bedroom, slamming the door behind her.

Baba just stood there wondering what was the matter with her.

I'm drunk, so what? he thought. *Why make such a big deal out of it? I was drunk when she met me. That day Kančeli and I had gotten drunk three times and sobered up three times, and she considered that entertaining, and now she's having a fit over it. I don't get it, I haven't changed, but she…*

Baba shook his head back and forth like a boxer who'd been KO'd, and imagined himself as Billy the Kid in that scene where Garrett recommends he get out of New Mexico because Garrett was soon going to be the sheriff of Eton County.

"How does that feel?" Billy asks.

"Like times are changing," Garrett says.

"Times maybe," Billy says, "but I don't."

Another night, Baba stuck his hand under Vera's nightgown and touched her thigh. Vera had gone to bed earlier. In the dark, silent room, Baba, obsessed with desire, had been turning over in bed restlessly, back and forth, back and forth. Vera wasn't asleep yet, she lay there tensely, holding her breath, like a pickpocket in flight, hiding in a doorway, waiting, listening, and then Baba's fingers found her. Vera froze.

And now we have an almost mythic situation. But not the one where Zeus disguises himself as a drowned cuckoo bird, and Hera takes him sympathetically into her arms and warms him at her breast, after which Zeus returns to his real identity and rapes her. Vera and Baba passed this phase long ago. Now we have only the cuckoo bird busted, Baba, who's gotten under Vera's nightgown and is poking around her underwear, kissing her. Vera didn't resist. She just imagined she was somewhere else far away, on some steep, deserted street, the facades of its buildings clean, stark, and it's dusk, and at the end of the street there are neon lights showing a fluorescent saxophone, and red, fancy letters next to it, and Vera, under the influence of the walk and the ozone, thinks how nice it would be to stop for a coffee at the end of the street. Or, since Baba had by now made his main move, that she was one of those blow-up dolls, or an actress in a porno movie, or that she needed money to resolve some terrible…to resolve Baba. So far, all Baba had penetrated was something dry and cramped from fear and disgust; had kissed clenched, cold lips. Vera's eyes skittered out into the darkness as she waited for the pain to pass.

And then it did, and the sperm caked up—Baba had long ago fallen asleep—and Vera continued to lie there awake, staring into the darkness. She felt relief. Or something like it. Like when you get a rotten tooth pulled. All that remains is the memory of the pain.

10. How Kančeli first yelled aaaaaaa-ha! and how he later met a referral officer

All morning long, Kančeli had been fiddling around in the apartment. An indeterminate fear, some horrible premonition had gripped him. He tried to get rid of it first by dusting. That didn't take long. There was hardly anything in the apartment for dust to collect on. Then he washed his dirty laundry. That didn't take long, either. The clean pants and T-shirt he spread out on the clothesline on the balcony and lit a cigarette. The horrible premonition was still with him. Actually, it was more a tension than a premonition. An excess of energy. He threw himself on the floor and started doing pushups. Forty, fifty, sixty, motherfucker. The tension hung on. He got into the shower and stood for a long time under the cold spray. Nothing. All that happened was he got a minor hard-on. He began to masturbate, but without any particular enjoyment, not even thinking about it, like it was routine, the way a sailor pulls on his rigging. The tension increased. He began to circle frantically around the room, inhaling and exhaling deeply, adding after every exhalation a loud AAAAAAA-HA! AAAAAAA-HA! AAAAAAA-HA! Čombe peeked out from the flowerpot, wondering how he had managed to get involved with so many lunatics. And then Kančeli stopped in front of the sliding doors and looked over the newspaper clipping. Center for the Prevention of Addiction, Red Cross, Friendship Park, Jarun.

And here he was in front of the Red Cross, smoking and staring at the bell tower of the Church of the Holy Mother of Freedom. An appropriate moment for some kind of epiphany and other exalted things, but Kančeli wasn't thinking about God, or the Holy Mother, or freedom. He was nervous, felt like a traitor, an asshole surrendering voluntarily. He regarded the entrance doors from a distance. That guy there, was he a porter or something more? Who could know? He lit another cigarette and walked back and forth, trying to create the impression that he was waiting for someone. Some official from the Red Cross that he was having coffee with and so forth. Yeah, that's why he's here at this ugly place. For love, stuff like that. And then that final scene from *The Wild Bunch* appears before his eyes. When those guys spend the night with the whores, boozing all night long, and then the next morning one of them says: "Let's go!" And another one says: "Why not!" And then the shit hits the fan.

"That's what you call *cojones*," Kančeli mumbled, put out his cigarette, passed by the porter, climbed the steps to the second floor, and entered the waiting room to the Center for the Prevention of Addiction.

The waiting room was eerily deserted. He sat down on an orange plastic chair and waited. These plastic chairs, they're the same in every waiting room in the entire universe; they're probably intended to give people a feeling of security. Like, wherever you may be, you can always feel at home in the waiting room. Or: Our waiting room, your place under the sun.

Shit, Kančeli thought, *check this out. A whole army of addicts roaming around outside, armed to the teeth. And here it's empty. Nobody anywhere. Like the plague just passed through.*

He sat there five, ten minutes in this spooky silence, and then he started having problems. Began to shake. *Run,* his brain hissed to him, *run before it's too late, get out of here,* and Kančeli got up and headed toward the exit, but he wasn't fast enough. A door opened before him and a man with a pinched, ashen face appeared. "May I help you?" he asked.

Kančeli looked around, as though the waiting room were packed and he were unsure whether the man was actually addressing him, and the man stood at the door, looking past Kančeli, thinking about God knows what.

"Alcohol," Kančeli said finally.

"Come in," the man said.

He sat down at a table piled high with files and gestured for Kančeli to sit on a vinyl-upholstered couch.

"I'm listening."

Kančeli stared at the cabinet in the corner where, on a blue coverlet on the top shelf, there lay displayed a pink shell—as though it were a precious gem—a plastic rose, and the photograph of some woman.

Thus far, the official had regarded Kančeli with a complete lack of interest. *What a guy,* Kančeli thought. *Spends his life in this hole, at this table, with his newspapers and his Lotto tickets, happy as the devil. It's enough for him that he's not like me.*

"So," said the man in a tired voice.

"Don't have much business here, do you," said Kančeli, buying time.

The man shrugged his shoulders indifferently. "I'm listening," he repeated, and the expression on his face indicated he didn't give a flying fuck about what he was going to hear.

Kančeli realized this and experienced relief. *Okay,* he thought, *we'll play hardball, like the pros. Like I'm in deep shit, and you're going to save me. We'll have a nice little talk, and then assume our positions.* So he told him an abbreviated version of his story. After hanging out all his dirty laundry in front of him, Kančeli was standing firmly on the ground once more, his initial nervousness and discomfort gone.

"You know," the man said, looking him in the eye, "I'm actually an expert on heroin addiction, I'm just on call here today, but—"

"I see," Kančeli said, interrupting him. "Sorry to disappoint you, but I don't happen to have any experience with heroin or hard drugs; I'm just a big time boozer. What I could do," he said, continuing, "is go out and get myself re-qualified and come back here in a month or two, what do you say?"

The man ignored Kančeli's bullshit and said that the Center was only the first step in the battle against addiction. And added that it was a positive thing that Kančeli had confronted the illness on his own initiative, and a few more phrases from the medical jargon, and then directed Kančeli to the Department for Alcoholism in Vrapče.

"We just do referrals here," said the man as he escorted Kančeli out. "The psychiatric clinic is purgatory, and it's up to you whether you end up in hell or heaven."

Aw, suck my dick, Kančeli thought, *that'll send you straight to heaven.*

11. Glazed eyes and the usual places of refuge

Bent over the sink, Vera was gently shaking a colander full of pumpkin blossoms. Although she had never eaten pumpkin blossoms before, she had the feeling she would like them. *Fried pumpkin blossoms. What kind of taste do they have? And if you can fry pumpkin blossoms, then why can't you fry rose blossoms,* she thought. *Or lily blossoms, or magnolias, or narcissus, or tulips. What a bouquet that would be on the plate!* She shook the damp blossoms out onto a dishtowel and noticed how the droplets of water glistened on the frail blossoms, wondered whether she should salt them right away or wait until they'd dried. The cookbook hadn't mentioned a word about that. It was something she needed to think about.

At that moment, Baba stumbled out of the bedroom. It was early afternoon. Baba mumbled something in passing and went into the bathroom. Vera got goose bumps.

First there was a powerful stream of urine breaking the quiet surface of water in the toilet bowl. Vera sprang over to the radio on the window shelf and turned it on, but it was too late. The first plop of shit had already plunked into the toilet bowl. A wave of disgust hit Vera full force; she sat down, trembling, in the chair.

"Oh my God," she said, holding her stomach with her hands, fighting off the nausea.

No, Vera's not a puritan, you've already figured that out, she just knows that the plunk of shit into the toilet bowl is a significant indicator of intimacy between people—all bathroom sounds in general.

Baba never tried to muffle these sounds from Vera, hide them by coughing and so on. Actually, it hadn't taken her long either to become comfortable where these issues were concerned. It doesn't take long when people are in love. What's the sound of an ordinary piece of shit plunking in the toilet bowl mean to people in love? Nothing. White noise. Like blackbirds cawing, dogs barking, or the sound of rain on a linden leaf. A reassuring sound confirming the presence of a loved one. And woe to all who begin to register this sound with the ear instead of the heart. The first time your stomach turns at the plunk of your loved one's shit, it's all over. Time for someone to pack his bags.

After overcoming her nausea, Vera considered what to do. First, she turned up the radio. Then she threw the pumpkin blossoms into the garbage. Then she sat back down and waited for Baba to come out of the bathroom.

"Wow, Manu Chao," said Baba as he buttoned his pants. "What are we celebrating?"

"Your departure, Baba," said Vera.

"My departure?"

"Yeah."

Vera's eyes, not her words, were what pierced Baba. She looked at him with glazed eyes that lacked the slightest hint of emotion. Just two precise optical devices, that's how to describe Vera's eyes.

"I'm not going anywhere," he said, looking off to the side.

But there was nowhere left in the apartment for him to avert his eyes. Wherever he looked, his eyes were already there, hiding from Vera's eyes. Refuges exposed, worn-out apologies, that's all Baba had left in this situation.

"Then I'll leave."

Those same eyes. This was no fucking joke. Baba tried to stay calm.

"No. Nobody needs to leave."

Vera started laughing hysterically. "We passed that point a long time ago, my dear."

And again, those dead, frozen eyes.

"Why in the fuck are you looking at me like that?"

"Take off, Baba! Get your stuff and go."

12. The old woman with the tired poodle, the alto sax, and eyes the color of a fresh hematoma

Kančeli had a good view of the world from his apartment—the present, the future, the whole picture. He didn't need to read newspapers, watch TV, or listen to prime-time news to figure out what was happening or what kind of world he was living in. All he needed to do was go down nine floors and walk through the neighborhood.

The people he came across that morning proved nothing had changed, that today was just like yesterday, and that tomorrow would be worse. *The guy sitting motionlessly on the bench there, in the shade of the dwarf oak trees, what hell has he been confronted with this morning?* Kančeli wondered. *More bills in his mailbox? A broken oven he has no money to fix? An empty refrigerator and growling in his stomach, the only music he's heard lately? Or the old woman walking the tired poodle, what's she thinking about? The mistakes she's made in life and when it was exactly that everything went wrong? Or maybe whether it is better to prepare dog meat in a stew or under the broiler. And the girl passing the old woman, in the bell-bottoms molded to her ass, is she aware she has just made contact with her future? Does she have any idea what awaits her? No way,*

Kančeli thought, *because if she did, she wouldn't have such a determined spring to her step.*

This is what Kančeli was thinking as he walked toward the marketplace, oblivious to the fact that his dramatic scenarios were pure literary affectation.

Nothing out of the ordinary had happened this morning to the man on the bench; he'd done his shopping, leafed through the newspapers, had a coffee, and was now waiting for friends with whom he planned to play cards. And the old woman was just recalling the face of a boy from long ago who always used to play Charlie Parker records in the student dorm; now she wasn't able to sharpen the image of the boy's face in her mind, but it seemed to her that the clean, clear sound of an alto sax was wafting out from somewhere, from behind an open window, from the heavens. And as for the girl, she couldn't imagine herself an old woman in her wildest dreams, and the distant future was even less on her mind. She didn't even see the old woman with the poodle. At the moment, even a fire engine siren would not have gotten her attention; she was rushing to the drugstore to buy a pregnancy test so she could bring an end to the suspense and uncertainty.

Meanwhile, Kančeli wasn't concerned about any of this; he just kept his story going. He put together a list of things that drew people's attention away from a bug in the grass, the ones we lived with, acid rain, and so forth. *Biblical prophecies draw our attention,* he figured. *We wait for the Horsemen of the Apocalypse to appear in the heavens, to ride up on their colorful horses, but they passed through these parts a long time ago. A horrible judgment has been pronounced, we just don't know it. Because, my friend, we have better things to do, more important things.*

Soccer competition between Dinamo and Hajduk

The Queen Mother's birthday

New face creams, detergents, and Kotex with those side flaps

Pamela Anderson's silicone boobs

Plastic surgery and chemical experiments on the skin of that (allegedly) white fag

Life and death of Princess Di and all the other princesses and princes

Troubles and romantic problems of the pathetic losers from Beverly and other Hills

And other important things without which our lives would be empty, dreary, miserable.

"Hey, Kančeli!"

Kančeli turned around, springing to the side.

"Your legs are working pretty well," Vera said, watching him admiringly.

Kančeli exhaled.

"Fuck, Vera, I know you don't like me, but are you're trying to kill me?" he said.

"Who, me?" Vera asked. "Where do you get that from?"

"I mean, coming up on me like that while I'm thinking," said Kančeli, hand on his heart.

"Oh, I just saved your life," said Vera. "If I hadn't interrupted your, uh, deep and profound thought processes, you would have walked out in front of a truck or something, you know?"

Kančeli frowned. "I don't know how Baba puts up with you," he said. "I wouldn't be able to do it for a single second."

"Okay," Vera said. "So let's go have a farewell coffee."

"Farewell?" said Kančeli.

"Hey, we spent almost a whole second together and now you're leaving me, but before you say your final goodbye, the least you can do is have an unforgettable cup of coffee with me, for old times' sake."

Kančeli peered at her suspiciously.

"My treat," Vera said.

Kančeli was doubtful.

"You don't have anything important to do that can't wait, do you?" Vera said.

"Okay, what do you want," Kančeli asked her after they had agreed that the pizzeria, Asterisk, had the best coffee, even though the fish smell from the neighboring fish market was a little too strong.

"Why do you think I want something more?" Vera said. "Maybe I just want to have a coffee with you."

"I doubt it," said Kančeli, yawning.

"Do you have a problem covering your mouth when you yawn?" Vera said with interest.

"Excuse me," said Kančeli.

"If you gave this some serious attention," Vera said, "and, let's say, taught your child to cover his mouth when he yawned, then in about three hundred years it would happen spontaneously in your family, it would be a completely natural action."

"I don't have problems like that," Kančeli said dryly.

"That fish market really does stink," Vera said, realizing too late that her comment about raising kids was off-limits.

"That's what you want to talk about with me, raising kids and how the fish market stinks?"

"I'm leaving Baba," said Vera.

Kančeli's brain analyzed and mulled over this information. And when the process was over: "Shit, what does that have to do with me? Tell Baba, don't get me involved in your—"

"Take it easy," Vera said, interrupting him. "What are you getting so excited about?"

"I'm not excited," said Kančeli nervously. "I just don't understand what that has to do with me."

"Because you're his best friend," Vera said. "Or do I have that wrong?"

Kančeli was silent, scrutinizing a pink smear on Vera's cup.

"And because I've told him a hundred times already, and he pretends like he doesn't hear me. And I really don't want to throw his stuff out the window, you know, in order for him to realize I'm not joking."

Kančeli looked Vera in the eye and saw something, a shadow or something similar that gave Vera's pale, green eyes the cast of a fresh hematoma. And he realized that Vera wasn't looking for a shoulder to cry on or someone to spill her guts to (for that she certainly wouldn't be turning to him, Kančeli concluded), but for a fire escape, the shortest way out of the situation in which she found herself.

"Is it that bad?" he asked.

"Yeah," Vera said, "and getting worse."

Kančeli didn't say anything. It wasn't necessary. He absently watched two sparrows scuffling over a piece of bread in front of the bakery. He didn't notice Žac and Jajo gesticulating behind Vera's back, signaling that they'd be in the cafeteria having a beer.

"At first he interpreted my silence as permission," Vera continued hoarsely. "And when I started complaining about his drinking, he acted like I was being a bitch. Now he doesn't even want to hear about it. I don't know."

The sparrows flew off, each in its own direction. Žac and Jajo moved off, around the corner.

"And what am I supposed to do now?" Kančeli asked.

"Talk to him," Vera said.

13. A gift from Allah, the G spot, and a typhoon with a man's name

The city summers on the fortieth-something parallel, it's a windless day, and the inflammatory mixture of nitrogen, oxygen, carbon dioxide (and lead and sulfur, not counting those substances the dumpsites emit when they're burning garbage), has been plaguing him since early morning.

A crazy, sick day. Like everything is taking place in the muffler of some truck. An ideal day for committing suicide. Or for a major binge consisting of a mixture of cologne water and pure alcohol. Everyone was off the streets. Even the shadows had retreated into cellars and air-conditioned spaces.

Kančeli and Stjepan are sitting in Kančeli's cave. The windows are closed, the blinds down, but the heat is still beating down on their heads, and they're panting like dogs.

"I went to the park to play a round of cards, and nobody was there," Stjepan said, as though trying to justify dropping in at Kančeli's unexpectedly.

"No problem, Štef," said Kančeli, "you're not interrupting anything."

"My retired pals don't even think about coming out of their dens on days like this," said Stjepan, wiping off his forehead with the palm of his hand. "Afraid their heart's going to give out. Who knows? Like they have something to lose, and years and years of life still ahead of them."

"How about some tea?" Kančeli asked.

"Black, no sugar, if you've got it," said Stjepan.

"Coming up."

"Is Čombe here?"

"Haven't seen him today."

"Then he's home, probably hiding out somewhere. You know, I'm not afraid of death. Not at all. What can I lose? Nothing. I've lived pretty long, seen a lot, survived two wars, three governments, as many fistfights as you can count. I don't owe anybody anything, don't have anyone to mourn my passing. People are stupid to let the past bother them. I have no past. In the morning, I wake up and say: okay, this is a new day, let's enjoy it! I sailed on a boat with a Malaysian guy. He had a lot of unusual proverbs. One of them I remembered. It goes like this: every morning at dawn Allah gives us one day, and it's up to us what we do with it. I like that. Who cares about what happened yesterday. Memories just gnaw at you, like cancer. Let's just make use of today. Let's have a nice conversation with someone, have a few laughs, drink a glass of good wine, you know? That's how to live life. And that's why I can still get it up; I take care of myself."

"I believe you," said Kančeli.

"That doesn't matter," said Stjepan. "I mean, whether you believe me or not. The only thing that matters is that I can still get it up."

"You got that right."

"And then I've got Magda, lives in that building by the gas station. She's almost sixty, but still a knockout. The only problem is that my little buddy's sort of unpredictable, you know, gets an attitude in the middle of the night sometimes, stands at attention when he damn well feels like it, then just stays like that for fifteen minutes, a half hour, and then I have to figure out a way to get Magda over to take care of business."

"I hear you," said Kančeli, offering him a cup of tea.

"You better believe it. And if she's not home, then I take care of him myself. But not without a little assistance. I've always got some cassette at home, the normal kind, you know, not with animals or stuff like that. The girls in the video store know what I like. And you're still living here, huh, like, in a cave?"

"Well, yeah," said Kančeli.

Stjepan sipped his tea and looked around the room. "You're right," he said. "If you give it a little thought, most of the stuff we have we don't even need. When I was on the boat or in the barracks, I had a lot less stuff than you have here, and I was fine, I didn't miss anything. I could do without it all today, everything but the telephone."

He was silent for a while, just sipping his tea. "Sex," Stjepan said, breaking the silence, "the reason women leave us is usually because the sex is bad."

"Some women, maybe," said Kančeli.

Stjepan gazed dreamily at the slivers of light penetrating into the room through the little gaps between the blinds.

"All women," he said. "You can fumble around in there all you want, but if you don't hit the G spot, you're done for."

Kančeli smiled. "What's with the G spot stuff?"

"I've got it down," said Stjepan. "I hit the G spot bull's-eye every time. I've got a sniper working down there. The only thing is," he continued sadly, "my little friend has gotten sort of fucked up, he doesn't listen anymore; we've got to come to some kind of agreement." He stopped, unsure whether to come out and say what was on his mind. "You know, the other day I found this little booklet with exercises—some rituals, you know. It's stupid, but since I've been doing them, it seems like the little guy has been a lot more obedient."

And Baba, meanwhile, was roaming through the deserted city like a prophet. But he wasn't looking for ears to listen to him, only the car he'd left in town the other day. At least that was his intention when he'd headed downtown, but now he wasn't even sure of that anymore.

What am I doing here? Why aren't I home? he thought. *Shit, everything*

*has gotten so ridiculously complicated. Everything always turns out differ-
ent than the way you planned. Instead of being home with Vera, or stretched
out on a beach somewhere, I'm walking around in this junkyard. Shit. This
thing with Vera is not a trivial thing, it's fucking serious. But it's not because of the drinking, that's for sure, why would it be because of that? I'm
not one of those. So what if I have a whiskey from time to time...ah, no
way, that's not the problem...She's dissatisfied with herself, that's what it
is. They're screwing her over at the university, she's working like a horse,
keeping the whole department going, and they won't give her a promotion,
that's what it's all about. Those big shots over there, shit, they're a bunch of
thieves. Just a bunch of arrogant kiss-asses, conniving and dangerous; they'd
run over their own mothers to get ahead, so why not Vera? And then it gets
passed on to me: I've given up, I don't write anymore, she's my only refuge...
Who does she think she is? Of course I'm not writing. I'm fighting for my
fucking life. What would we be eating if I weren't working at Agramer?
We can't even pay the utilities with her salary. Says I need to go, she can't
stand the sight of me anymore. Well, don't look at me. Fuck her. Close your
eyes. No one needs to look at me.*

He found sanctuary underneath the train overpass and tried to
come up with a plan. Nothing. He couldn't concentrate. The blood
was pounding in his ears. And then a hissing. And then other sounds.
Oh God.

He kept walking. Maybe he ought to drink something. Okay, he just
needed to be careful. A beer or two, no more. So he doesn't fall asleep
in the streetcar or something and have problems again. Like the other
day. An earthquake had awakened him; he didn't realize someone had
grabbed him by the shoulder and was shaking him roughly. He came
out of his deep sleep and saw this gaping mouth above him, babbling
something at him. He didn't even realize what was fucking happening.
It was too much information all at once. He just gawked at that face,
those blubbery lips flapping away, exposing big yellow, horsey teeth.
He thought: *Where did this head come from? Where am I?*

And the Head just kept on blathering, like a wound-up clock.

"Ha," Baba said, looking around.

"...this...hotel...," was all Baba could decipher from the Head's harangue.

"What do you mean, hotel? This is a streetcar, a fucking streetcar. What in the fuck am I doing in a streetcar?"

And pushed the Head away, shambled out, and looked around in panic. Nothing at all was clear to him. The crowd in the streetcar was staring at him, giving him that syphilitic look. Smirking. *What in the fuck are they looking at?* "Fuck off!" "Go to hell!" No, today he'd be wiser. Just one beer. Maybe two. He wasn't going to let a bunch of Neanderthals make fun of him. *Fucking trolls!*

And Magda, she's not feeling the heaviness of the polluted afternoon heat. She's just eaten, nothing heavy, just fresh, salted cucumbers and tomatoes, it's not the time of year for pork or stuffed cabbage, no. And now she's sitting in the chair opposite the fan, looking like she's riding a bike. Her hair waving in the breeze, squinting, lips clenched, just riding into the night, and nobody can stop her. Magda can hardly wait till night comes, but not because it's going to cool off. There won't be any cooling off for a while, the humidity is going to continue, and people with heart problems have to be careful—that's what they say on television. Thank God there's nothing wrong with Magda's heart. She's just racing on into the night, because a person has to have a goal in life, a destination to make it to, and Magda is pleased when she makes it till noon, evening, night, a month, a season, and God willing, a certain age. Sometimes she makes it to her daughter's place in Samobor, but not often, and less as time goes on. She also makes it to Stjepan's, but not with a feeling of unfettered joy. *Oh, God, no way. That man, that impossible man.*

She met Stjepan last summer. It was the hairdresser's fault, that is, the newspapers in the salon. They were on the top of the pile, and Magda took them and started to read the advertisements. An ordinary, silly notice in that column: Pensioner, lives alone, seeks someone to have coffee with, movies, long walks, something like that. The meeting place was Mondays at 10 a.m. on the terrace of the Utrine marketplace cafeteria. So he can be recognized, he is going to be carrying a black cat. A BLACK CAT? Magda thought it was some kind of joke, someone's idea of a good laugh. People don't carry around black cats in order to be recognized. Ridiculous. However, the ad obsessed her for days, she couldn't stop thinking about it, so the following Monday at a quarter to ten she passed by the cafeteria terrace. She usually didn't go to the market on Mondays, it was the worst day to go, but since it was right here in the neighborhood, why not?

He was at a table at the edge of the terrace, a cat in his lap, a big, black cat. Magda recognized him by sight; he often sat with friends in that park over by the school. Playing cards, drinking, talking, wasting time. Magda didn't have much of an opinion about them. *Bunch of bums*, she thought, and as she entered the market area asked herself why he was looking for company when he already had company, and maybe that wasn't even the guy who put in the ad, maybe he just happened to be there. But the cat! It's him, no doubt about it. He was still sitting there when she came out of the market area with a green salad in her bag—she had to buy something, she thought, so she wouldn't look like she'd come because of the ad.

Magda didn't need more people in her life; she already had plenty. She had a lot of acquaintances in general, so this wasn't really the best time for making a new one.

But her friends weren't particularly exciting, there were no unexpected surprises or new experiences when they met; the best thing they could do for her would be to leave her alone, not call her, not come over to visit. All they did anyway was talk nonsense. Told her it was impossible to make new friends; at their age, all they did was lose the old ones, wasn't that absurd?

And they'd repeat it, as though it were an incantation, and they believed in it, her old friends, and they stuck together. The only thing that put a little pizazz into their lives was death. So Magda preferred to be alone. It was more exciting for her to watch the sky change color in the west as evening fell, or the lights of the neon signs in the market place reflecting off the trees than it was to sit with some friend and rehash old stories, much more exciting. At the same time, she longed for a new companion. She wanted to meet someone she'd always look forward to seeing, you know, someone who'd make going to the marketplace a real adventure. Time flew by imperceptibly with people like that, the days were shorter, and you slept much better at night. Magda and that person would discover one another, over a coffee or something, and in time be able to reveal the most intimate of details to each other, all the things we say only when we talk in our sleep.

And that's why she went over to Stjepan's table that morning, holding the bag with the salad tightly in her hand, and said: "Good morning. Is this chair free?"

How careless she'd been, God, like a teenager.

A man like that, with a black cat in his lap, it wasn't a good omen, and she, almost throwing herself at him. As though she hadn't been brought up to avoid everyone and everything and, especially, her own feelings. First her parents, then her husband, *God rest his soul*, they all filled Magda's ears with the same stories about abstention, that noble virtue. And the worst thing is, she held to it, the submissive woman. Stood by while life and all its spectacles passed her by.

She was like those old island women who had never swum in the sea, for years and years. And then a typhoon showed up, lifted her off the ground, and dropped her right in the middle of the deepest ocean. Stjepan. It was nice in the beginning. Stjepan told interesting stories about the sea and faraway harbors, he was polite and all that, and then one night he'd lifted up her skirt and stuck his face where man had never gone before, you know, and Magda was so shocked that she forgot all the lectures about abstention and just dove in with Stjepan, to the bottom of the deepest ocean, and God, even months later she still couldn't figure out which emotion dominated: guilt or satisfaction.

And Magda was no longer afraid of her own feelings. At least not like before. The first time's the hardest, right? It just sort of got on her nerves that Stjepan treated her the same way he did those girls from the films, those call girls. And now, at the end of another day, as the ventilator hums its tune and the sun sets behind those high-rises near the marketplace, Magda asks herself whether Stjepan will call this evening. And what she will tell him if he does. Okay, she can say she won't come, find yourself another fool. But isn't it a little boring to say "no" your entire life?

14. An ultramarine blue piercing and what the mosquito poison killed

Robi had to show Suzi to someone. How does it go: it's no fun to ball if no one knows you're balling. Okay, Robi hadn't balled her yet, but that didn't matter. He had to show her to someone.

From the beginning, he had held no high hopes. He didn't dare to hope for anything, at least anything serious, not even when she invited him over to her place one day. He thought, *she's just being nice to me because I saved her from that guy.*

But now, after she'd come to the bookstore three times, *Jesus, a girl like that, an actress, and also smart,* and so on, he finally realized he was in the game, and he was burning with the desire to show her to someone. Friends. Robi didn't have many friends and those he considered friends weren't in town. Everyone was at the coast, scattered all over. And he'd be closing up the bookstore in a few days and heading for the island of Krk. He and Suzi, *Jesus, what a picture that will make.* He already imagined the scene, he and Suzi having a cocktail at dusk on the terrace of his parents' villa in Baška…and here the scene stops. His mother, it dawns on him. What is he going to tell his mother? She definitely won't approve of him bringing Suzi. Robi cringed. *Suzi's a little too open for Mama,* he thought, *too direct.* His mother expects him to settle down, not with a particular individual, but with "a member of a good family."

"An actress, interesting," is what his mother would say. "And what are your parents, what do they do? What part of Zagreb do they live in?" She would immediately ask.

Robi banished that horrible image from his mind, and as he left the bookstore with Suzi, a thought occurred to him: *Kančeli! I'll show her to Kančeli. He's in Zagreb.* He'd get in the car right away and go to Kančeli's.

Kančeli was glad to see them. Hearing a knock at the door, he expected to see Stjepan with another discussion about G spots, but instead he saw a pretty brunette, six chilled, half-liter cans of beer, and Robi. Not bad, all things considered.

Some terrible mistake has been made, he thought as he let them into the apartment, *if a girl like that is hanging around with Robi.* And he was glowing like a fucking comet. Came in strutting like a peacock, dragging his hunk of burning love in behind him.

"Are you his cousin or something?" Kančeli asked the brunette, as she walked languorously over to the window and began to stroke the marijuana leaves.

"Isn't this illegal?" she asked, looking askance at him.

"Everything that's entertaining is either illegal or unhealthy," he said.

"Or both," she said.

"You got that right. I can see the two of us are going to get along just fine."

Robi pretended he wasn't paying them any attention. Sat down on the couch and opened a beer.

"As you can see," Kančeli said, turning toward Robi, "there's no electricity here or anything else to divert our attention, so let's just get to the crux of the matter, which is beer."

"What do you mean?" she asked.

"Well, TV, stereo, stuff like that," he said. "They just spoil the party."

"We didn't come to party," she said.

"You didn't? Then why did you come?"

"I have no idea," she shrugged. "Just for the hell of it, no reason."

"Okay, that's cool. Want to try some of my summer harvest?"

She nodded silently, so Kančeli brought a tray full of dried buds from the balcony.

"This is going to catapult you into the heart of the Milky Way," he said, filling up a clay pipe.

"And you don't mind not having a TV?"

"No."

"You don't miss anything, movies, sports…"

"No."

"Nothing at all?"

"Maybe snooker on Eurosport."

"Snooker?"

"Yeah, I like to watch them play. It calms me down."

"What direction is Morocco?"

"Morocco?"

"Yeah."

"Somewhere over there, I think. What do you care about Morocco?"

"I'd like to go there and hear those drummers."

"Drummers?"

"Drummers, musicians. Have you heard of the Jajouka musicians?"

"I don't think I've heard them."

"You don't think you've heard them?"

"I've forgotten everything."

"I don't get it."

"Drinking, blackouts, and so on."

"Aha. Sometimes I lose an hour here or there, too."

"And see, I've lost years and years."

"But that's okay."

"We'll go to Morocco later."

"Okay."

"Find your musicians."

They were on the third pipe when Čombe sprang into the room. Suzi and Robi were sitting on the bamboo couch, and Kančeli was sitting on the floor, leaning back on the couch, hitting off the pipe. They were already seriously loaded.

"Come here buddy," Kančeli said, calling the cat over, but the cat just walked over him and nestled in on Suzi's lap.

Suzi dreamily stroked the cat as she watched a plane circling above the marketplace, ejecting mosquito spray.

"I have an angel cunt," she said suddenly, not addressing anyone in particular.

"Oh yeah?" said Robi. "What kind is that, an angel cunt?"

"Oh, it transforms people into angels," she said.

"You hear that, Kančeli?"

And Kančeli doesn't hear anything. He's sitting on the floor in a cloud of smoke, smiling.

"Check this out," Suzi said.

She moved Čombe out of the way and lifted her T-shirt. Robi saw a belly button piercing, a tiny ultramarine bead.

"You see that, Kančeli?" said Robi.

And Kančeli didn't see anything. Sat in a cloud of smoke, taking hits from the pipe.

"And you should see my thong panties," Suzi said.

And Robi said nothing, just reached for the pipe, and Kančeli gave it to him without resistance, with an expression on his face like an orgasmic Chinese hamster.

Suzi took a beer from the bamboo coffee table and sprawled back onto the couch. Čombe had no complaints because Suzi continued to gently stroke his body with her other hand. Then Suzi wrinkled her nose. She picked up a strong smell of mosquito spray. It sort of ruined her mood.

Yeah, actually, why did we come here? she thought. *So you could show me to your friend? So you could both check me out, grope me, make some decision, evaluate me or something?*

"I saw Baba the other day," Robi said.

"I know," Kančeli said.

"How do you know?"

"He told me."

"What did he say?"

"Who?"

"Baba."

"Oh, you know Baba, he always has stories to tell. Said someone sank a boat, I don't know where, and then the cops showed up..."Then he became silent, welded to the edge of the couch.

I don't know if it's because of the weed, Suzi thought, *but I feel like getting it on. You know, just rolling around like a pig. Except how am I going to get it on with him,* she thought, looking toward zoned-out Robi. *And that other guy,* looking at Kančeli, *I don't know—Kančeli, what kind of a name is that? Italian?*

"Show us your thong panties," Kančeli said, emerging suddenly from his torpor.

"Yeah," Robi said as he handed the pipe to Suzi, "show us."

"No," said Suzi, instinctively pressing her knees together, and the cat opened his eyes, wondering what was happening.

"Bitch," Kančeli said. "You think just because you're wearing Palmers underwear…"

"The tiny mini-panties," Suzi said coldly, "Palmers are for grandmas and conservative female politicians."

"What's wrong with Polynesians?" said Kančeli, who was flashing at that moment, who knows where his head was (and meanwhile, he had gotten hungry).

Suzi suddenly relaxed and smiled. The barbed wire she had erected just moments ago against the guy with the weird name transformed itself suddenly into silk. "Come on, have a little," she said, offering her beer to Kančeli.

He refused the beer, but squeezed himself in between Suzi and Robi on the couch. This was too much for Čombe. He slid off Suzi's lap, annoyed, and sauntered into the kitchen.

"Let's see what it says here," said Kančeli, taking Suzi's hand and moving his thumb over her palm.

She didn't resist, but as soon as Kančeli started speaking, her blood ran cold.

"Oh, we have a Sagittarius here. No goal is too high for this girl, she aims for the stars and even further."

Suzi got goosebumps. *HOW IN THE FUCK DOES HE KNOW I'M A SAGITTARIUS?* "And I see," Kančeli continued, "I see a hundred of your faces. A hundred, but different ones, get it? You pretend, you like to change, cover your tracks…once you sold shoes, you also danced in a night club, and then…actress, you're an actress, and you believe you'll—"

Suzi pulled her hand out of Kančeli's in panic.

"WHAT THE FUCK IS THIS?"

"Got it right, ha?" Kančeli asked.

Suzi looked at him in disbelief. *Yeah, he got it right, the moron.* Suzi often dreamed about a role, some supporting role, nothing special, in an American film (but it didn't have to be American). So what, if a girl who was selling newspapers at traffic intersections just yesterday can be the world's top supermodel today, why can't she, Suzi, a second-year drama student, get some little role in an American film? Suzi began every day with the same prayer: "Five minutes, I just need five minutes, a few good lines, and the doors of heaven will open for me." She wouldn't have any complaints if Brad Pitt were in one of her scenes, give Suzi someone to exchange her magic and chemistry with. (Brad Pitt, accepting the best actor Oscar: "I wouldn't feel right without mentioning the brilliant Suzi, who inspired the entire crew, and especially me, with her amazing acting and energy, whose cameo in this film has the power of an atomic bomb, and honestly speaking, makes the entire film. Thank you, Suzi, wherever you are, I love you, I love you." The camera zooms in on Angelina Jolie in the audience. She's got a dumb smirk on her face.) *Five minutes,* Suzi implored, *just a lousy five minutes and you'll get what that stupid Marilyn would've gotten if she'd been smarter and fucked normal people, not the president of the United States.*

Even Kančeli wasn't without desires, but his were based on age and experience, and they told him that Fate did nothing but screw people over, and that desire went something like this: the lower you aim, the less disappointed you are. So his aspirations lacked all glamour and pretense; they were concentrated solely on the imminent future, the one that could be measured in minutes, or hours at the most.

At the moment, he just wanted to get into Suzi's pants. And thought he knew how to do it.

"How did you know?" Suzi asked him after she'd pulled herself together.

"What?"

"That I'm a Sagittarius."

"I didn't know," Kančeli said, "I just guessed."

"Are you bullshitting me?" she said.

He shook his head and lit a cigarette with the operatically inclined lighter.

"Cool, huh?"

"Robi," Suzi said, not registering the fact that the lighter was playing "Für Elise." "I'm sure he told you I was studying drama."

"Robi didn't say anything," Robi chimed in, stretching and taking a hit from the pipe. "Robi's not a snitch."

"Want me to tell your future?" Kančeli asked.

"No way," Suzi said, shuddering.

"You're right," Kančeli said, "we won't do that, because all you'll hear is a bunch of crap from an old, ill-tempered, and, by the way, very stoned son of a bitch."

Suzi needed a time-out. What was happening here? What kind of guy was this Kančeli?

"Let's make some coffee," she suggested.

"I'm out of gas," he said, pointing toward the camp stove in the corner of the room. "How about if I make a move on you instead?"

"Whatever," she said.

"I'm no prizewinner," Kančeli began. "I'm old and fucked up. My apartment looks like shit, as you see, and so does the inside of my head. I have no ambition, no steady job, no money, and no possibility of inheriting any, so I have nothing a decent woman can grab on to. And that's the catch."

"Yeah, that's the catch," Robi echoed back.

"A woman your age," Kančeli continued, "is usually attracted to what a man is going to mature into later—and then is disgusted by it. I've got a surplus of those things. I survive from day to day, no plans, no reserve future; I don't hide my emotions up my sleeve. You know this already. I'm everything your parents aren't. And that's why I've got a chance. Because you're still young and you know there's no possibility you'll end up marrying me."

"What are you babbling about?" Suzi asked.

"I'd like to check out that angel thong," Robi said as he slid from the couch onto the floor.

"Everything I've said so far," Kančeli said, flashing again, "about my present circumstances and the billboards with your name on them in front of the Zagreb theater, as well as the fact that that is real lapis lazuli," pointing to her navel piercing, "certainly doesn't mean you can't get it on with me."

"That's right," said Robi.

"I know this is bothering you, don't think I don't know, that I'll be reading tonight by the light of the kerosene lamp—check out this poetic scene—and that fireflies are going to be swarming onto it, dirtying their wings, but that still doesn't mean you're not thinking right now: fuck it, why not, if I don't do it now, I might regret it the rest of my life, thinking I missed something fantastic, amazing, unfuckingbelievable. And you're not such a goose that you'd allow yourself to give guys like me a single second's thought later on, so you'll just go ahead and ball me and resolve the dilemma, am I right?"

Suzi was silent. She was in a foul mood again. *This homegrown stuff is definitely a bummer. And this old guy's probably never even heard of Ecstasy. What he is, is a dinosaur.* And then she went back to not liking him again. Robi didn't seem interesting to her anymore, either. Suzi frowned, wrinkled her nose, and sniffed. The smell of mosquito spray was getting stronger and stronger. The weed and sex aroma was gone. The mosquito poison had killed it all. She sat there stiffly, waiting for Robi to get moving.

No big deal, Kančeli thought, *just another stupid afternoon.* Not the first or last in his life. He stared into nothingness and waited for them to leave.

15. The lost anchor and the red umbrella

dear vera,

i don't think what you wrote me was depressing. i just don't think it's some kind of croatian specialty what's happening to you, baba, kančeli, and the others. things are bad for people all over the world, and the end result is we're all just trying to live longer (and better) than the others. i'm having my own hassles right now; the only good thing is that from my perspective, none of you has aged. you know? when i think about the zagreb years (our fucking youth!), i put on the clash, open a beer, and see us all there in front of the quasar, and i'll be damned if that wasn't the best drug in the world. no, i'm not mourning the loss of my celebrated youth, but, fuck it, i love to reminisce about it. when you're young, you hang in there or you crash, or you just squirm. that's the whole story. we were so stupid thinking that we'd settle down as time went on, find a firm anchor to hold on to, sail on in. shit. now it seems like there are no anchors, that something like that doesn't even exist. or that i've lost it somewhere and now i'm just floating, in some zero gravity space with nothing to hold on to, and no idea how long it's going to last. probably until i get sucked into that black hole.

stop.

now that we've reconnected, our life mission isn't going to be mourning all the lost opportunities and thinking about the good old days. come on, don't. when wasn't it good? all the days were good, and especially today, we're breathing, eating, walking down the street. at any rate, i got stuck playing at 78 speed. never got married, but lived for years with a girl from thailand (long live multiculturalism!) and then she figured out she had better options. luckily, there were no kids in the picture, all we had were two dogs and they both went to me. now i've got the status of an undesirable bachelor with two old dogs, but i don't have any regrets. and how about you and baba, do you have kids? stupid question. with or without kids, breakups are tiresome and fucked up. like hangovers, except hangovers don't last as long. my advice: if you have pets, make sure he gets stuck with them. i like what kančeli did. not the drinking, family, and job, but that he lives like a hermit. that's one of the better ways to spend the rest of your life. really, why do we need all those things we insist on accumulating? books we don't read, records and CDs we don't listen to, a bunch of plates we never eat from. whatever the case, kančeli definitely isn't crazy, and he's got a lot of balls. he always did. just remember how he used to talk to that cop when he'd crash our parties in the bar, like he was talking to the bartender. i remember once, we were in some café and some racketeers burst in, three huge montenegrins, and they forced us all away from the counter. and we all went, kančeli was the only one who stayed. and when they asked him what the fuck he was waiting for, he told them: boys, you've got a problem. what problem? one of them asked. the problem that you're stronger than me, but i'm still not afraid of you. and they left him alone there, drinking his beer. anyhow, coffee in a can is a thing of the past. it's late afternoon here. dreary and rainy. i see a red umbrella on the street. wonder what's underneath it. i'm going to put on the clash now, have a beer, and dance.

take care, tom

Vera shivered as she read the mail, imagining Tom dancing in some room with a beer in his hand, alone, on the other end of the tangled web that transports these messages, and "The Cool Out" is blasting from the speakers. Imagined him as a twenty-something-year-old. Couldn't imagine him as a forty-something-year-old. She found a photograph in her album of Tom and her at some party, hugging and smiling. Tom had a joint in his hand, and you could see the edge of the table and the neck of a bottle, probably beer. Weird. We just accept other people who aren't around anymore as they appear in old photographs. But not ourselves.

"What does that person have to do with me?" Vera asked, peering at herself in the photograph.

Then she took a beer from the refrigerator and put on the Clash—"1977" blared from the speakers. Beer in her hand, Vera bopped over to the mirror in the hallway. Guitars were rocking out in the background, and Strummer was belting something out about heaven, and Vera was standing there with a beer in her hand, gaping dumbly into the mirror. *What does that have to do with me?*

16. Ghost photographs and the heart of a lioness

At certain exceptional moments, really exceptional, a six pack and some cigarettes can radically change someone's life. Plus condoms.

It's so weird, Elza thinks, *how the most trivial things can shake us up and cause us to do something we'd never have done otherwise in our wildest dreams. If it hadn't been for those two, I could easily have slaved in this tin cage for the rest of my life.*

Elza was moving. All afternoon she'd been packing her stuff and now was walking around the apartment checking to make sure she hadn't missed anything, passing through the living room, registering the white rectangles on the wall where posters of Azra, Springsteen, and ten photographs had still been hanging this morning.

Elza wasn't connected to this apartment anymore. When she'd put the last thing in a box, the apartment stopped being hers, and she stopped belonging to it.

Now she gave closer attention to those empty rectangles. Didn't they somehow summon up the spirits of the photographs that had hung here? A photo from Mljet had been on the wall, and above it, a wedding party picture, and then the bigger rectangle, that had been a photo of Elza's husband in uniform, taken at the beginning of the war. Elza's husband believed in the war and what they said on TV—that the war was just and so forth. It didn't occur to him that the war was being waged so the new gang could throw the old gang out of the villas that the gang before had thrown the Jews out of. Elza hadn't believed in the war, and she was terrified. Then her husband died during an attack on some unit in Petrinja. He died, and Elza stopped trembling and began to suffer. Lost in her own private hell, she would be overcome by guilt and tears every time she would let some man get close to her. And then the time came for Elza to stop suffering. She had sustained other blows as well. First, getting fired from the bank and then again from the boutique where she was working off the books, and then months without a job, living on her savings, plus the constant feeling that she was contagious. That's how they acted toward her, with that overbearing politeness, avoiding her. *Watch out, her husband was killed!* Or even worse—pity. She'd come over to a group and the conversation would stop, and everyone would give her that look, like she was retarded. Elza couldn't get over her loss because everyone was always reminding her of it. *Elza, you know, the one whose…*But she coped very well.

Her frail body and her 5 feet 7 inches, approximately, don't reveal anything about her heart. At least not to people that have no conception what the heart of a lioness is like, for example. And Elza was doing okay, found a new job in a tobacco shop in the Trnje district and had been there almost two years now. Two long years. She recollects her husband in a different way now, without all the dramatic colors and stormy emotions. It was a comforting image now, in soft shades, the picture of a man she once knew, and then he left because he thought he should, and that was admirable.

And then yesterday afternoon that yellow vw bug stopped in front of the tobacco shop and two people got out. Elza's attention was attracted by the girl's jet-black hair. *It's dyed*, she thought, *that can't be her natural color.* She bought six cans of beer and some cigarettes. Then they got back in the car, and the man came back and bought another pack of cigarettes and some condoms. Elza thought for a while about why they didn't just buy the condoms right away.

Did they forget to buy them, or was the guy just embarrassed? It doesn't matter, Elza thought. *This is what usually happens with young couples. Cigarettes, condoms, and beer. How many times had Igor and I...* and then Elza stopped, terrified. Listening to herself talking to herself.

Are the dead alive?

No.

And are the living dead?

Not yet.

And you, are you dead or alive?

I'm alive.

How do you know?

She became silent, stuck with the question for which she had no answer. And then Elza saw. Saw everything clear as crystal. *I'll sell the apartment, get in the car, and take off. Just get in the car and go, wherever.* The cards started falling into place. That evening she talked to the owner of the tobacco shop, and they just kept falling. One of his friends was looking for an apartment in New Zagreb, Zaprude is an okay neighborhood, the apartment's the right size...and as far as work is concerned, she could give Vienna a try, his relative was the caretaker of a nursing home, he'd give her the phone number and address.

And now Elza was walking around her bare apartment, impatiently waiting for the buyer, and unless he was some trickster or awful swindler, she would be sitting in some café in Vienna, and nobody there would be looking at her, giving her that she's the one whose husband look.

17. Performances in the park and bad timing

"Hold out your hands!"

A thirty-something-year-old woman with a raspy voice, craggy face, and penetrating eyes was standing in front of Kančeli like one of those maidens from the Nordic *Edda*. Voice, face, eyes—that's the order in which Kančeli became aware of her presence. The sound in the room traveled faster than the speed of light. And then came the philodendron in a white, glazed container in the corner of the room.

"Hold out your hands!"

Which of them was going to touch Kančeli: Urd, Verdandi, or Skuld?

"Close your eyes!"

A voice like that he could more easily associate with a bar than a medical file and a seal containing the keyword "psychiatrist."

Kančeli closed his eyes and saw all three: Urd seductively twined around a shiny copper pole attached to the counter of the bar, Verdandi smiling and pouring him a bourbon, and Skuld hovering beside him, stroking his thigh, and whispering the future into his ear.

"Your hands are shaking."

Of course they are, Kančeli thought, *but it's from fear.*

Shaking because when he'd been in the lobby of the Vrapče clinic, looking for the admissions office, he had entered by mistake a room with dirty, gray walls, and lying on one of those beds with wheels had been an old woman with a waxen face. Kančeli didn't realize the woman was dead. His brain had no time for details, it was floating in some gray-colored liquid, trying to locate its coordinates, figure out where he was, how he got here, other general questions. There was also a doctor in the little room, sitting at a table underneath the window, working on some forms. Kančeli's brain formed the question, "Is this the admissions office?"

"Yes," said the doctor without raising his head from the forms, "but for hell."

What is it with these people, thought Kančeli, *this is already the second time hell has been mentioned.* He was shaking because in the hospital park, hallucinations of extended hands had appeared to him, hands mumbling words he didn't understand. *What happened to their eyes, what kind of eyes are those, who hollowed out their eyes?* Kančeli's brain asked in panic. His hands rose in defense, pushing the hallucinations to the side.

That's why Kančeli was trembling. Shaking, actually, in fear that the two huge doctors were going to jump him, tie him up, and put him in bed. Keep him there for months, feeding him pills.

He told her that.

"Come on, pull yourself together," she said. "We don't have any beds to waste, you know yourself what condition our health system is in."

Kančeli exhaled. He knew what kind of condition the health system was in. He wasn't in that bad a condition. *I'm doing great compared to the health system,* he thought, encouraged by the fact that somebody, something, was in worse condition than he.

On his way back from the clinic, Kančeli swung by the Agramer office, but Baba wasn't there. He wasn't at home, either. He found him at the marketplace, in his usual spot.

"Man, Baba, I was just up at Vrapče," Kančeli began in a cheerful voice.

"No kidding," Baba said. "And how are the natives, are they in a friendly frame of mind?"

"You don't understand," Kančeli said. "I was in the hospital, you know, in the wing for alcoholics and so forth."

Baba raised his eyebrows. "Why?"

"For treatment," Kančeli said.

"Of what?"

"What do you mean," Kančeli said. "Drinking, what else?"

Baba observed Kančeli closely. He didn't notice anything unusual. Nothing in his behavior indicated that he was in an abnormal state of mind. That he'd gone off the deep end or seen an apparition of the Virgin Mary. He looked completely normal; he was just talking nonsense.

"You've gone nuts, man," Baba said.

"Listen to this," Kančeli said, taking from his pocket the file with his medical history and beginning to read: "anxious, labile, without signs of psychosis...denies abusing pills or heavy drugs...admits potus—What's that, potus?—in partial denial regarding problems with alcohol. This psychiatrist is a sow."

"The usual?" asks the waiter, nodding toward Kančeli.

"No way," Kančeli said. "Give me a black tea."

"I'll have another one," Baba said.

"That woman is a real sow," Kančeli continued. "Got on my case, that I don't know what alcohol does, that once I fall into its clutches... that people think it's easy to stop, and then die in the worst agony, that treatment is the only solution, a month in the clinic, and then outpatient treatment, plus AA...frigging nightmare."

Kančeli exhaled, grabbed a cigarette, and lit up. The lighter was cranking out "Für Elise" at full speed.

"Why did it occur to you to go up there?" Baba asked.

Kančeli took a deep drag, exhaled, and considered the smoke suspended in the air. Then he looked Baba straight in the eye.

"The other day I was drinking coffee out of Maja's cup," he said. "I figure that's the reason."

"I get it," Baba said. "But isn't it a little late for that?"

"That's my life story," Kančeli said. "Always late. You can't say I didn't do some things right, but it's my fucking timing. What are you gonna do?"

"As long as we're on the subject," Baba said, "what's with Maja, do you hear from her?"

Kančeli looked at his burning cigarette. "I can't even connect the name to the face anymore," he said. "Actually, I can't even remember what she looks like."

The waiter set down on the table a cup of tea and a bottle of beer. "Are you sick?" he asked Kančeli.

Kančeli wouldn't even look at him.

"And what are you going to do now?" Baba asked.

"Nothing," Kančeli said. "I threw the cup away."

"I mean the thing with the hospital. Are you going to get treated?"

"No way, no chance," Kančeli said, trembling. "Those people are fucked up. Actually, so am I, but their fucked up and my fucked up are two different animals. You ought to see their eyes! I've never in my life seen the whites of the eye so hideously clean, clear, and bright. How do they get them like that?"

"By drinking a lot of juice, probably," said Baba.

"No, seriously. They sit around over there cutting up pieces of colored paper, making collages together, like in kindergarten."

"You're not *really* going to stop drinking, are you?" Baba said in horror.

"Just watch me," Kančeli said. "This is the second installment of my failed life: Kančeli in the enchanted world of non-alcoholic drinks."

18. Sumatran cigarillos, spritzers, and straw hats

The bedroom's voyeur heaven. Bare floors, bare walls, a narrow, white dresser that goes all the way to the ceiling, a natural wood bed, and a night table with a lamp—nothing here to distract Stjepan's attention from Magda, who's getting dressed.

"I must be crazy going along with this," said Magda, turning her back to Stjepan. He was sitting on the bed, not bothering to hide his pleasure at watching her.

"Why would you be crazy?"

"To do what we're doing."

"What exactly are you referring to?"

Magda lifted the pillow and pulled her bra out from under it. "Having sex," she said.

Stjepan smiled. "What's wrong with sex? Sex is good."

"I've still gone crazy."

"People who don't screw go crazy."

"That's not what I'm talking about."

Magda put on her dress, turned, and faced Stjepan. "In that ad in the papers, it said you wanted company for the movies, to have a coffee, and so forth," she said.

"What are you saying?"

"Look what this has turned into."

"Well, that's okay," he said.

"Do I have to take all my clothes off?"

"God, yes."

"At my age…"

"What about your age?"

"The way I look."

"You look fantastic, like a forty-year-old."

"At least turn off that damn lamp."

"We're not children, Magda; we passed that point a long time ago."

Magda was silent.

"I've seen a lot of tits and ass in my life," Stjepan said, "and I assume my little friend isn't the first one of those you've seen, either."

"Oh, stop, would you!" she said, upset.

Stjepan held up his hands in the air. "Okay, okay."

"My deceased husband didn't like to do it with the lights on," Magda said.

That's why he's deceased, Stjepan thought. "We won't talk about that," he said, "let's talk about something nice." He got out of bed, put on his boxers and a faded sailor's shirt, and went into the kitchen.

"How about a glass of wine?"

Magda came in after him.

"And you just take everything as it comes," she said, "you don't worry about a thing."

"I don't have time for stupidities, Magda," he said. "I love life too much to waste it worrying about all kinds of nonsense."

Magda waved him away. "Is there anything you don't consider stupid?"

"Oh, yeah, a lot of things, very many things."

"For example?"

Stjepan thought about it. "Well, everything that helps you feel good."

"That's not an answer."

Stjepan shrugged his shoulders.

"It's strong," Magda said, taking a sip of wine. "You'd better make me a spritzer."

"That would be a shame," Stjepan said. "This isn't the kind of wine for a spritzer." He raised the glass to the lamp and watched as the light turned the liquid into a deep ruby red. Then he lit a cigarillo of Sumatran tobacco.

"Mmmmmmmm," he said, exhaling. "What could be better than a little sex, a glass of wine, and a good cigar? See, that's not nonsense."

"That's all you think about," Magda said. "I still want a spritzer," she added.

He got up, took her glass, and added a little faucet water to it.

"Should we go to Maksimir Park tomorrow?" he asked.

She gazed at him in surprise. He hadn't suggested going out somewhere together in a long time.

"What are we going to do there?"

"Oh, nothing in particular. Take a walk, have a coffee at the Lookout or in the Swiss House, just feel good."

"I don't know," she said.

"We can take a blanket and lie down in the shade somewhere near the lake," he continued.

Čombe sashayed into the kitchen.

"Hi, Čombe," Magda said.

Čombe meowed.

"See, you've even tamed him," Stjepan said and went into the hallway. He returned with a linen cap on his head. "I bought it yesterday. It's nice, huh? See it has this netting, so your brain doesn't fry in the sun."

Magda wondered what had gotten into him. She was sure it wasn't from the wine. He just stood there with the cap on his head, in his underwear and the wrinkled, striped T-shirt, a thin cigar between his lips, amidst a cloud of smoke. And smiled.

"I'm going to wear it tomorrow," said Stjepan, "and you take that straw hat. It looks good on you."

19. An ashtray, a naïve crow, and the art of gynecology

"Hi, artist!"

An icy gust from a menacing storm howled over Vera's lips and froze Robi's eyes.

Vera was going to the movies. She had a ticket for 9 p.m. and had no plans whatsoever for socializing, and then she spotted Robi in a café while walking around window-shopping at the Kaptol mall. Actually, her attention was drawn first to a girl with jet-black hair, like a crow, and then she realized uncomfortably that the very, very young, smiling, crow-black-haired girl was sitting with Robi. Vera didn't intend to pass up an opportunity like this.

"Hi, Vera," Robi said. "What are you doing so far from your stomping grounds? Are you going to a movie?"

His voice was cold because of the storm.

"No, I'm not, thanks for asking," Vera said. "May I?" she asked, gesturing toward the chair, which, it appeared, had been scribbled on by some Italian, "or are you having an important business discussion?"

The wind became chillier, and so did Robi's reactions. He searched for a sentence that would eliminate Vera, but he was too slow.

"No, not at all, take a seat," said the crow-girl.

"Thank you," said Vera, nodding her head graciously. "A coffee with cold milk and a mineral water," she told the waiter, who had appeared before she'd had a chance to settle into the chair. And then to the crow-girl: "I'll bet this is a café that replaces the ashtrays as soon as the first ash falls. Is there such a word, 'ash'?" she asked, turning to Robi, and then back to the young girl. "Robi's a poet. Whenever you have questions about linguistic nuances or complexities, he's the one to ask."

"A poet?" said the crow-girl, lifting her eyebrows.

"You didn't know," said Vera, pretending to be astonished. "The bookstore is just a cover-up for his many talents. Isn't that right, Robi?"

Robi shrank in his chair. It wasn't his night. He knew it the minute he saw Vera moving toward the table, and now he was certain, because the way things stood, the two of them were going to be in charge of everything, and he'd have the role of spectator.

"Vera Suzi, Suzi Vera," Robi said, trying to regain the initiative, at least a little.

"Has he published anything?"

Suzi didn't turn to Robi, she was asking Vera.

"Oh yeah, of course," Vera said. "He's published a few collections of poetry his mom was very enthusiastic about. But not only his mom. There are at least two or three other people that think it's poetry."

"He didn't tell me anything about that," Suzi said.

And Vera wondered whether the little crow was stupid, totally naïve, or just didn't understand sarcasm.

"Oh, Robi is very self-deprecating," Vera said. "Besides being a poet, he's also a contemporary artist, a kind of successor to Joseph Beuys. Haven't you seen the wall installation in the bookstore?"

Robi got up from the chair.

"Sit down, don't go; how can we hold our symposium about you if you leave?" Vera asked.

Robi fell back down into the chair. And Suzi's eyes bounced around in space, back and forth between Vera and Robi.

"What installation?" she asked, looking at Vera.

"That water pipe, the knife thing, and the toilet paper that are hanging on the wall," Vera said, "that's Robi's installation. Not to mention photography and film, two of Robi's other loves. Although his mom and the wider public have no clue about them."

Suzi looked at Robi sideways, and her curious expression told Vera that the girl had begun to comprehend. Robi gave her an ironic smile, but it didn't help him much.

"He didn't offer to get you involved in artistic photography, film, and so forth?"

Suzi shook her head no, impatient to hear the rest of the story.

"Well, of course not, you're still in the early stages," Vera said. "How long have you known each other, five, six days, right?"

Suzi nodded.

"Well, yeah," Vera said. "First you're just buddies, then he starts in with his poetry, then the art, and in the end, he's got you under the lens, legs spread, of course, like you're at the fucking gynecologist's."

Suzi giggled. "You're kidding, right?"

"No way," Vera said. "Robi, as an artist, holds a very specific, that is, gynecological view of women. That's his specialty. In the blink of an eye, he's got you in his web. Half of Zagreb jerks off to his art. What do you think Robi lives on? That bookstore?"

Robi got up suddenly, knocking over the chair.

"Slut," he hissed, "stupid whore, bitch. Are you coming?" he said, looking at Suzi.

She gaped at him in disbelief. "No way in hell," she said.

"Wait, where are you going?" Vera asked, "How can I attack you in absentia?"

"You're lucky I came along, girl," she said, watching as Robi left.

"Why?" Suzi asked. Her voice held a mixture of astonishment and curiosity.

"Why?" said Vera, surprised. "Because he's as stupid as a doorknob."

20. The worried threesome sitting in the shade of the dwarf oak tree, and things that should never be spoken about

It had been several days since Magda had disappeared. They spent a very nice day having a picnic in Maksimir Park, and then she disappeared. Stjepan kept calling her, ringing her doorbell, walking past her building, looking up at the windows, but all was in vain. And now Stjepan was upset, but not because Magda's disappearance had ruined his sexual life;

that was the least of it. Thinking it over, Stjepan replayed in his head various scenes from those films about murderers and maniacs, and that got him agitated. Very agitated. Thus far, only the thought that something bad could happen to him personally had disturbed him—that he'd fall into a stormy sea, or get a knife between the ribs in some bar he'd found himself in in the past, or slip off a ladder—and now he's disturbed by the thought that something bad has perhaps happened to somebody else. That's new for Stjepan. And that adds to his confusion.

Baba's worried, too. Worried because Vera doesn't scan him with her eyes anymore when he comes home. Baba'd finally concluded that Vera had come to terms with the situation, that she'd washed her hands of him. That's what his head told him, but his instincts told him something else. Some horrible premonition had taken root deep within him, and it could be interpreted something like this: it's all over for you, Baba; you fucked things up royally. Baba believes more in instinct than intellect. Realizes that it was instinct that had enabled the survival of countless species, while intellect, the pride of the human species, was responsible for most of the delusion and self-delusion. And was very worried about that.

Kančeli is also worried. Worried because withdrawal is going along very well. Nothing within him is rebelling; there's no raging beast inside howling for a drink. And that scares him. Kančeli lies in bed with just one thought: *Fuck, what if It wakes me up in the middle of the night, grabs me by the throat, drags me over to the tobacco shop in Zaprude, and orders me to buy a beer and drink it up, motherfucker, otherwise you're going in front of a truck.*

And so, all three of them, worried, are sitting on a bench under the dwarf oak tree, talking. About various things, just not about what's bothering them. That doesn't cross their lips. They keep that to themselves, hide it inside, no matter what it is they're upset about. That's the way it's done. If people start talking to each other about what's worrying them, start trusting one another, then the shrinks would have to close up shop. They'd have to wait tables off the books, or clean cages at the zoo, or starve to death.

And that's why Kančeli, instead of saying he's terrified ever since he gave up booze, that he's just waiting for the DTs to get him, is just keeping the conversation superficial, asking Baba what he's writing.

And Baba, instead of saying: Fuck this bullshit, why don't you ask me how I'm doing, why it's so hard for me to go home, and why Vera and I hardly ever talk anymore, said: "A novel, I'm writing a fucking combination war-soccer-thriller about a housepainter."

And Stjepan, instead of telling them both: Boys, screw that, Magda has disappeared, she's gone, and I'm really concerned about her, yes, I'm a hundred years old, but this is the first time in my life I've cared about somebody, and I'm going crazy with worry, I've been calling, looking for her all over the neighborhood, waiting outside her apartment building entrance, and now I don't know what else to do, said instead: "I don't know much about that; I'm not going to get involved. I just don't understand why people would even write about that kind of stuff."

Baba and Kančeli stared at him.

"I mean, what do you get out of it?" Stjepan asked.

"Out of what?" Baba asked.

"That writing," Stjepan said.

"People feel better when they read a good novel, I guess," Baba said.

"What are you, some doctor?" Stjepan asked.

"An engineer for the soul," Baba said, recalling the Marxist theory of literature.

"Really, what good does it do you?" Stjepan asked, not giving up.

"That's not what it's about," Baba said, disturbed by the unexpected questions.

"Then what?" Stjepan asked. "Can you make a living from it?"

"Rarely," said Baba.

"There you go," said Stjepan.

Kančeli stayed out of it, just making sure nobody played dirty.

"Do you feel better when you write some novel?" Stjepan attacked, sensing that his opponent was wavering.

"I don't know," said Baba tensely, "I haven't ever written a novel."

"Štef, didn't you say that book you found on the sidewalk helped you?" Kančeli interjected.

Stjepan regarded him disdainfully. "The exercises helped me, not the reading part."

"It doesn't matter, first you read them."

"Oh give me a break!"

"What exercises?" Baba asked.

"Forget it," said Stjepan, angrily waving him off.

They sat there silently for a while. The wind was murmuring through the dwarf oaks, the Canadian poplars, the birches, the ash. A woman was crossing through the park, carrying a cloth bag with a rainbow on it. In the distance, the siren of an ambulance could be heard. Stjepan became despondent thinking about Magda. *Where was she?* Baba was thinking about how he'd rather walk through a minefield than go home. Kančeli was trying to figure out how many hours he'd been alcohol-free and wondering when the crisis was going to hit.

"See you."

"See you."

"Bye."

Each went his own way.

Stjepan went over to Magda's apartment, rang the doorbell, knocked on the door, put his ear to it to see if he could hear sounds inside, sniffed to see if he could smell a decaying body, because he'd often read in the newspapers about people who'd died in their apartments, who weren't missed by anyone, and then the police and their neighbors had discovered they were dead by the stench of the decaying body, and now Stjepan was sniffing, putting his nose to the edge of the door, murmuring: "Fuck it, Magda, you're not one of those, you have somebody to miss you."

Kančeli went to the supermarket and walked along the aisles with the beer, wine, schnapps, whiskey, and cognac, and didn't feel anything out of the ordinary. No excitement, desire, need—nothing. Then he went to the Asterisk, ordered a large draft, and sat there staring at the mug. The bartender looked at him and shook his head, and when

Kančeli paid and left without even touching the mug, the bartender raised his eyes upwards, but there was nothing in the heavens to explain Kančeli's behavior.

And Baba avoided his high-rise like the plague, went to the Plaza café at the bus station, ordered a beer and a schnapps, and proceeded to get hammered.

Meanwhile, Vera didn't care what Baba was doing, whether he was getting bombed or helping some blind person cross the street. Something else was going through her mind at that moment.

> Dear Tom,
>
> It's little comfort to a person that he's not alone in his misery…actually no comfort at all, but that's not what it's about; it's the zero gravity (you really nailed that concept, good for you). I feel all the time like I'm living in some weightless state, and that the powers determining my Fate and which I can't control are so strong that they are capable of appropriating my life at any moment, wiping their ass with it, and flushing it down the fucking toilet. Ah, that's what I'm talking about, people who have lost control over their own lives. They think they're in control, but they're not. That's the major problem.
>
> You're right about those delusions that we're going to settle down as the years go by and drop anchor in some safe sea. Exactly, no such place. When I think about it today, it seems like we were more firmly anchored during our "wild" years than now, in our "more mature" years. What a stupid paradox. Were our feet more firmly planted on the ground then? Maybe we were nourished by the hope that we were going to achieve something in life, whatever that means, and that when we grew up, we'd collect all the threads and have a firm grasp on them. Well, I'll tell you, I don't have a firm grasp on anything.

My job at the university's not secure; they can fire
me whenever they feel like it, and nobody would even
blink an eye (the situation there is that every male is paid
better than I am, no matter how useless he is or even if
he was hired two days ago, and I've been there almost
fifteen years).

At any rate, who cares about my translations or my
texts about writers from Scotland or New Zealand? If
I give it a little more thought, everything I do is completely pointless. A seamstress sews a dress, sells it, and
gets paid; the woman who buys it is happy she has such a
pretty dress. There's a point to that story, and everyone's
satisfied. But how about my story?

I don't know, but it seems like I'm not able to make
any significant decisions by myself anymore. And I'm
not critical at all now of women who accepted the role
of mother and wife and allowed the husband to steer
the ship. If they were lucky enough to find a more or less
normal guy who doesn't go overboard with the bullshit,
then more power to them. They can just relax and wait
for the end to come.

I chose the other route, and now I am where I am.
You're right, we live in good times. Things aren't boring; on the contrary, everything's fucking exhilarating, a
heavy mix of classical drama, horror, and thriller. Except
sometimes it's good to settle for something a little
lighter, some love story with a happy ending.

Man, it's so hot here, it's like I could set my lungs on
fire every time I take a breath. So I'm going to try to
pretend I'm not here, that I'm floating on some iceberg.

Vera

P.S. I don't have a beer in my hand anymore when I
listen to the Clash.

EDO POPOVIĆ

EDO POPOVIĆ

21. Children's names, peed-on pants, and a hidden coin

Water was boiling in a stainless steel, cylindrical cooker. Ninety-six, ninety-seven, ninety-eight…The whole burner was vibrating to the rhythm of the stainless steel geyser…and ninety-nine and one hundred. An even one hundred degrees Celsius, the red switch announced with a sharp, authoritative click. Barefoot Suzi, carrying a cup containing a mixture of instant coffee, sugar, and milk, glided over to the cooker and poured boiling water into the cup.

How stupid, she thought as she read the words Electro-Petra on the bottom of the cooker. *Why not Electro-Petar? Electro-Suzi. Jesus, Suzi. Further proof of how selfish and cruel parents can be, giving their child a name like that. Suzi! Like a bimbo from one of those teenager serials.*

Children's names, she felt, ought to be temporary—like the belly button, or even better, the hymen—and should only be valid until the loss of virginity, after which everyone gets to choose his or her own name. And then Suzi wouldn't be forced to lie throughout her puberty and say that Suzi is short for Suzana. Or even worse, that it's a nickname. You know: my real name is Kaja, with a Y. My mom adored Marley, went to several of his concerts, one of them in Dortmund in the 80s. I was conceived there; my mom was stoned out of her mind, still can't remember today who knocked her up.

Suzi wasn't ashamed of her little fibs. Why should she be? All she'd done was assuage the injustice for which she had not been responsible. Actually, she wasn't lying about the father. She didn't know who her father was. And her mother, for some reason, didn't want to tell her. Was she protecting Suzi from some evil? Or herself from unpleasant memories? It wasn't important to Suzi anymore, if it ever had been.

As she drank her coffee, she looked out at the façade of the building across the courtyard, overgrown with ivy, and the hall of the judo club. Every night she heard sounds of bodies hitting mats and muffled screams coming from it. The view Suzi had from the kitchen had changed often while living with her mother. The Pula arena and the sailboats were her first memories. She also remembered the harbor's

90

hydraulic lift in Rijeka and the gas tanks in Krk. Then the bus station in Karlovac, and the chimneys and ironworks in Jesenice, the train tracks in Munich, the bakeries in Trešnjevka. Her mother never stayed for long in one place. She was afraid she'd get stale, rot. Die of boredom. Literally. There's nothing nicer than to see a new face in your bed every morning, or at least a different view through the window, she would say. In time, the new views, new faces, and her mother's philosophy made Suzi nauseous. She just wanted to wake up once, look through the window, and not have to ask herself where in the fuck that tree under the window came from. *Where am I now?*

When she registered for drama studies, Suzi decided she wasn't going to let her mother choose the view from the kitchen. Then, her mother had gone to Frankfurt with some Bosnian guy, chosen some other view. Suzi picked the one overlooking the judo hall near the mosque. And she didn't die of boredom. Okay, true, the view from the kitchen never changed. But at least a new face appeared in her bed once in a while, although that was nothing much to brag about.

There was a little bit of variety, but inside, most of them were pricks, Suzi would say some day in an interview, if she were given the opportunity. *At that time I was just looking for a little attention and understanding, and all I got was dick. That's literally all I got. It seems that's the ultimate a man can offer a woman. How would I define men? I just did. Creatures incapable, for the most part, of understanding what their wives say to them. You tell them something, and they give you that look, thinking: okay girl, say what you have to say so we can get it on. You know? I finally came to terms with it. I thought, fine, the world's not perfect, it is the way it is, but as long as that's the way it works, I'm going to at least pick the time, place, and position.*

"I don't know," Suzi said to Vera later that day, "but Robi seemed to be worth the effort."

They were sitting on the terrace of the Zagreb movie theater, and Suzi was talking about her episode with Robi. Suzi often felt that whatever she was saying served only as background noise in the ears of whomever she was talking to. A humming that gives them time to think about what they're going to say, which usually has absolutely nothing to do with what she just said. It seemed as if people didn't even converse anymore, that they long ago lost the capacity to listen to one another, and now all they do is tell their own personal stories. A bunch of manic monologues, that's what communication's boiled down to. With Vera, it was different. She felt like she was talking to Vera instead of an ashtray. She felt it that night at Kaptol mall; that is, that Vera was the kind of person who knew how to listen.

"I mean," Suzi said, seeing the question in Vera's eyes, "he didn't jump me immediately, feel me up, and so on."

Vera nodded, and said that in general it was a good sign when a guy didn't start raping you immediately.

"He was over at my place—it was sort of weird, you know, that he didn't show any interest in me. And then he'd freeze up every time I happened to touch him. I thought, okay, the guy's a little shy, doesn't want to make the first move, needs some time to feel comfortable, wants us to get to know each other a little better, whatever. I've never met anyone so...weird, I don't know. And then that friend of his—Kanc and something."

"Kančeli," Vera said.

"Yeah, that's the one," Suzi said.

"The guy living back in the Stone Age," Vera said, smiling.

"I wonder," Suzi said, "how he can live in that apartment."

Vera didn't answer, just sat there silently for a while. Some hustler was circling the tables, a guy with slicked-back hair, in a blue, short-sleeved shirt with dark circles of sweat under the arms. Vera was thinking how stupid it had been to unload her problems on Kančeli, and Suzi was torn about whether she ought to be baring her soul to someone she barely knew.

"And Robi, is he really mixed up in pornography?" Suzi asked. "I mean, it just doesn't go somehow with his behavior."

"He doesn't have anything to do with that," Vera said, "I just made it all up."

Suzi looked at her in disbelief.

"Why?"

"Because," Vera said calmly, "it sounds better than the real problem our Robi has."

Suzi was shocked. "What, he's not some rapist, is he?" she asked.

"Not as far as I know."

"I've read about cases like that," Suzi said, "guys that are like cuddly teddy bears in the beginning, but when they make their move…"

"His mother," Vera said.

"What?"

"His mother's the problem."

"What happened to her?"

"Nothing. She just turned him into an idiot."

"Good day, ladies," said the hustler frenetically, as though he were on speed, "I'm sorry to interrupt your conversation, but allow me to show you something which will make your lives easier."

And shoved under their noses a set of knives. They had no reaction whatsoever. Actually, they looked at him as though he were a wasp trying to slake his thirst in a little beaker, and then immediately put him out of their minds.

"He's forty years old," Vera continued, "and his mom still tells him how to live his life. Picks out his clothes, friends, you know, and even worse, tries to control his choice of girlfriends."

"You're kidding," Suzi said, goggle-eyed.

"Seriously," said Vera. "Our Robi is like one of those video game characters. And his mommy's holding the joystick."

"Unbelievable," Suzi said.

"And he just listens to her, doesn't say a word. One of my friends went out with him a long time ago, before the war, when we were still students. Robi took her home to introduce her to his parents. They're, like, a very distinguished family. Live in a villa on Tuškanac. His father was a diehard Communist who managed to do very well for himself when democracy came along. So Robi takes her to be introduced, and the old lady makes a big production—who are her parents, what do they do, why does she dye her hair, why does she have rips in the knees of her jeans, what kind of T-shirt is that—a real circus. Duda just went with the flow, looked at Robi first, and…nothing. He just stood there staring at the ground. So she told his mom to shove it up her ass and took off. Like that."

"Shit," Suzi said.

"Yeah," said Vera.

"And what you said about the poems…"

"That's true. He's published a few worthless books of poetry. He could have published whatever he wanted, mama took care of every-thing. Actually, he studied art, had a few shows. The bookstore's just his toy. He'd starve to death if it weren't for his parents."

"Depressing," Suzi said.

"Yeah, depressing," Vera agreed, and asked the waiter for the check. "Want to walk me to the tram?"

"Are you married?" Suzi asked as they walked to Jelačić Square.

"Yes, but no," said Vera.

Suzi smiled. "What kind of answer is that?"

"We live together, I mean Baba and I, but we never signed any papers."

"Hm," Suzi said. "What's that like?"

"What?"

"Really living with someone."

"I don't know," said Vera. "It's impossible to manage something like that with Baba. I mean, really living."

"He's probably not the type of guy who jumps your bones imme-diately," said Suzi.

"He's even worse," said Vera.

A terrier tore past them and chased away the pigeons walking around in front of the Hotel Dubrovnik. "These dogs," Vera said.

"Is he good in bed?" Suzi asked.

"Who, Baba?" Vera smiled. "Yeah, he's great in bed; he doesn't snore and doesn't fall asleep on my side of the bed…"

"That's not bad," Suzi said, giving Vera a conspiratorial look, "I mean, for a man."

"No, it's not," Vera said. "And what's even more important, Baba has the courage to admit it when he pees on his pants."

"That he what?"

"Pees on his pants."

Suzi snickered derisively.

"There's nothing funny about it," Vera said. "That's a man's worst nightmare. Most men would rather confess getting it on with a man than admit to peeing on their pants. Very few men are capable of that. You know, they go to the bathroom, and sometimes they manage to piss on themselves, and then they make a big production about it. One of my boyfriends climbed out the bathroom window on account of that. Just fucking took off and didn't call for days."

"That's something I haven't experienced yet," Suzi said cheerfully. "At least I don't remember anything like that."

"Don't worry, there's time; you will," Vera said. "Just check them out when they come out of the bathroom, and you'll see how totally bummed out they are if there's even a little drop or two in the zipper area. It doesn't matter if it's water. They think the whole world is fixated on their zipper; mankind in its totality is contemplating the origin of those spots on their pants. But not Baba, no way."

Suzi couldn't stop snickering.

"It happened to him on our first date. He came out of the bathroom dead calm, spattered all the way to his knees, and I asked him if it was from washing his hands, and he looked at me like I was crazy: what do you mean, washing my hands? he said. I pissed on myself."

"At least he's honest," Suzi said.

"Yeah," said Vera.

But only when it doesn't matter, she thought.

And Baba, tense, agitated, and unaware that a conversation about him pissing on his pants was taking place just five hundred meters away, was walking along Masarykova Street. Vera had been in a good mood that morning, as though everything was tip-top, as though he hadn't come home wasted the night before, as though he had gone to Punta Arenas and would never be returning. Even drank a coffee with him and happily told him how she had lured the girl away from Robi, how Robi went ballistic, and what he said to her. And then, as the morning went on, Vera got silent, and everything went back to the way it was before...mute, mute.

Baba was entering the bookstore, and Robi greeted him with a phony, insincere smile.

"How're ya doing, Baba?"

"Never better," said Baba, "never better."

"Not too many people can say that for themselves these days," said Robi.

"'Cause they're like pigs who love wallowing in the mud. People aren't happy when things are going well."

"Interesting way of looking at the world," said Robi, wondering what brought Baba to the bookstore.

"So, Vera's a whore, slut, and so forth," Baba said, depriving Robi of the chance to give it any further thought.

Robi assumed a defensive expression. "Sorry," he said, "you know I didn't mean it like that. She came up and just started giving me shit out of the clear blue sky."

"Doesn't matter," Baba said. "Why are you apologizing to me? Why are you apologizing at all? If you were to apologize for your rotten poems, well, I'd accept that. But you're apologizing for the only sincere thing you've done in your life."

"So what do you actually want?" said Robi, irritated. "You like playing the role of hero protector, right?"

"I won't pretend I like you," Baba said.

"This sounds like the beginning of some—"

"All these years," Baba said, interrupting him, "I put up with you because of Kančeli. Because he, for some idiotic reason, saw potential in you. Imagine!"

"Make it short, Baba. I don't have that much time for you."

"No problem, I'll make it short," Baba said dryly. "You know, Vera did you a favor getting that girl away from you."

Robi turned pale.

"She just spared you all the agony you'd have to put up with later from your mother," Baba said.

"Fuck off," Robi hissed.

"Tell me honestly," Baba continued maliciously, "do you and your mommy fuck like mother and son, or in the normal way?"

"Fucking lush!" Robi screamed.

"Excellent," said Baba. "You've finally spoken one true word. You're improving."

Leaving the bookstore, Baba didn't feel a bit better. He was still agitated and angry. As children, they'd often played that game with a coin and three matchboxes. Where's the coin. And no matter how hard Baba would try, how much he wanted to figure out the box the coin was hiding under he'd pick up the wrong one every time. His rage increased with every new attempt, and it was directed at the box. Just like now. True, Baba couldn't stand Robi, but he wasn't the one hiding that coin. He definitely wasn't the one.

22. Living with someone isn't the same as getting AIDS

Kančeli liked his job at the carwash. No people there with eyes like fish, no fish stench or swarms of metal-green flies. Just water and soap. Water spraying and the smell of suds. A clean job. The conversation he had had with Vera had been replaying in his head the last few days. Put him in a bad mood every time he thought of it. *Fucking promising to hand deliver his good friend's head. Why did he agree to something like that?* He should have refused Vera. Let her deal with Baba by herself.

Anyhow, Kančeli thought, gesturing to a silver Citroen (or is it a Renault) to pull up a bit closer, *what am I supposed to tell Baba?*

He angrily attacked the hood, rear windows, and fenders of the car with long sprays of liquid artillery. What could he even say to him? He gave one last spray to the rear windows and watched the car disappear into the tunnel, urged on by sprays of water and the yellow strips of a rotating mangle.

The woman driving it, he thought, *probably had a wild youth. Listened to Patti Smith and Zappa. Wore* FUCK OFF *pins. Partied by night and slept by day. And then, the fairytale came to an end. Now she's an assistant in some ministry, proud of her natural blonde hair, carries a purse worth three hundred dollars and something, drives a shitty Citroen or Renault, and doesn't have the guts to tell her husband to get the fuck out of her life. And I'm supposed to tell that to Baba! To get the fuck out of Vera's life. Listen, Baba, I had coffee with Vera the other day, yeah, coffee, and, uh, Vera says to pack up your stuff. Why? Well, probably because things got too screwed up, I don't know...fuck it, Baba, that's the way it goes. Risks of the job. You should've figured out by now that living with someone isn't the same as having AIDS; once you get that, it's all over, it can't be fixed. If you ask me, don't complicate matters, get your stuff and leave. I can tell you from my own experience that the first few years are the hardest. Afterward you adapt somehow, later you don't feel the knives in your gut.*

Stjepan, his ear glued to the door of Magda's apartment, had a similar sharp-knives sensation in his gut. Like some horrible acid gnawing at his stomach. There was no sound coming from Magda's apartment. All he could hear was the irregular beating of his own heart.

"Are you looking for someone?"

Stjepan stepped back, embarrassed. A meter away stood some granny with a Pekinese on a leash, and Stjepan cursed silently that he hadn't heard them coming up the stairs in time.

"Hm, yes," Stjepan said. "Magda, I need Magda."

"And you are?" the granny asked suspiciously, looking him over.

What should he tell her? That he was Magda's friend? Stjepan and Magda's relationship couldn't really be characterized as friendship, could it? It wasn't friendship they were talking about during all those phone calls. Holding the receiver in one hand, and trying to maintain the little guy's erection in the other, that wasn't what you'd call an act of friendship.

It would be closer to the truth if he said he was servicing Magda, but the granny wouldn't understand. *This topic*, Stjepan thought, *just isn't really a topic that can be discussed anymore.*

"Friend," said Stjepan. "I'm her friend."

"Hm," said the granny, snorting. "Friend? If you were a friend, you'd know she was at her daughter's in Samobor."

Stjepan refrained from taking this wonderful woman and her gorgeous Pekinese in his embrace and bestowing on them both a big kiss.

"Well, I haven't been in Zagreb for a while," he said.

"Her daughter got hit by a car," the granny continued, not even registering Stjepan's transparent lie. "In the pedestrian crosswalk, imagine that!"

Stjepan couldn't recall the last time he'd gotten such marvelous news.

"Luckily, she wasn't badly hurt, but somebody has to be with her and the child, men you can't dep—"

"A beautiful dog, ma'am," said Stjepan as he headed down the stairs.

23. Anarchism, cash, and Big Brother

dear vera,

not good, i mean the tone of your letter. it seems like you've fallen for all those success stories, let other people determine what's important and what's not.

i don't know, but if i were in your place, i'd give this some thought. there are always forces you can't control (ideology, politics, money, fashion, whatever), but you can choose whether to get involved. at one point we harbored the illusion that we could oppose the power of the party and behaved accordingly. we had everything then, except freedom (at least that's what i believed). freedom was in the hands of the party, and we made up for that lack by blathering about anarchism, fucking our brains out, getting loaded, and listening to loud music. did that destroy communism? no. what destroyed it was money we didn't have, and money wasn't important to us. we were just farting into the wind, as johnny štulić would say.

things are a little different today, now we have this freedom, right, but we're still depressed. we've got these fucking thieves who are more privileged, richer, freer than everyone else. you can snivel all you want, but that's the way it is. in canada and in croatia, throughout the entire free world. of course they've fucked us over again. the same ones who destroyed communism and endowed us with freedom. for years they terrified us with stories about big brother's ideology coming from the east. bullshit! big brother is cash, pure cash, and it comes from the west.

so what do we do now? participate in it? sit and cry? fight? i don't intend to do any of the three. it's clear to me that the buck can only be defeated by bigger bucks. so i just ignore it all. don't give a fuck. i have all i need, and i don't need a lot. i don't want to need a lot. if you look at things that way, life becomes a lot easier. that is, you can do whatever you want with your life. try my recipe, believe me, it's a good one.

greetings, tom

"Your recipe's nothing but a bunch of shit," Vera murmured as she read Tom's message. "And so are you. Like you Canadians say: you're full of shit, Tom."

Dear Tom,

Nothing you wrote makes a bit of sense. You missed the point. I'm talking to you about feelings, and you barrage me with a bunch of jargon from Sociology

101. What in the hell's wrong with you? I know all that stuff about ideology and money, I know who brought down the Berlin Wall and why, and what people mean when they talk about freedom (or love, Carver, see how bright I am), I fucked against Communism (with you, you might recall), and I've done and tried everything… And you're giving me a lecture as though I were some Canadian inbreed living in the middle of nowhere.

Okay, it's not completely your fault, I'm also to blame, because I wrote you in code, didn't call things by their right names, and I apologize for that. And, what I really wanted to tell you is that I am furious because I've begun to take on the qualities I used to hate in others.

The other day I met a great kid, she's studying drama, and she's really pretty and smart. And then I realize I'm lecturing her. I was supposedly trying to protect her from her environment, forcing the experiences of a mature woman upon her, my fucking experiences! Horrible. I've lost my mind. Like I was never twenty-something, like I didn't consider women in their forties grandmas then, with only death to look forward to. Okay, the parameters of youth are fairly flexible, they move as we age, but still. Interfering in someone's life, expecting someone to bypass the most exciting part of it, the part where you learn from your own mistakes… All my mistakes, from this perspective, were really romantic little adventures, and I'll be damned if I wouldn't love to do it all over again. Don't delude yourself, you were also one of my mistakes (Baba, too, but it wasn't his fault he became my destiny), but that isn't important. What's important is that I apologize to the girl right away.

Then there's Baba. We haven't been speaking for quite a while. He does his thing, I do mine, nobody listens to the other. Baba's drinking like a fish, which is nothing new, he was always like that, but what is new is that I'm not going to put up with it anymore. And what do I want? Not that much, just an hour or two a day I can devote to myself. With Baba that's impossible. He's like a cancer that's metastasized and spread throughout my body, devoured me, and all I can do at this point is excise it. I've wasted so much time and energy in his depressing mindspace (which has meanwhile become our common mindspace), and now it's time for me to spend however many more years there are the way I want. Doctor, am I normal? That's what I was trying to tell you. It wasn't about the global situation, it was about the situation in my living room, my head. (Now I'm thinking, why am I hassling you with my problems, but still, I'm not obligating you to do anything. Why would I? I could just as well send this to one of the addresses that send me junk mail, it would get there. It's just important for me to blow off steam somewhere and the monitor is a great listener, and actually, I'm still going to think about whether I even want to send this.)

Greetings, Vera

Vera pushed away the keyboard and looked over the message. *Actually, what did this have to do with him?* she asked herself. *What does it have to do with anybody? I'll just save it as a draft, go take a shower—by then I'll think of something.*

24. Watch out, friend, for a high-heeled blonde with big, crisp bills in her hand

In Utrine you can buy Turkish T-shirts, jeans from Sandžak, Montenegrin cigarettes, Macedonian wine, pot from Hercegovina,

Colombian cocaine, Kosovo heroin, Austrian frankfurters; you can buy anything you want there twenty-four hours a day, anything but a common container of cooking gas. Frustrated by this, Kančeli set out for Zapruđe for the smelly gas. In front of the bank in the business center, he ran into a long line the likes of which one would sooner expect to see at a lottery outlet or a soup kitchen.

Some pensioner is probably in there, trying to do some heavy juggling with his account, Kančeli thought, making his way through it. *These pensioners*, he thought as he approached the bank display window, *it's pure magic what they're able to do with their retirement money.*

He peered into the window and recognized the woman from the silver Citroen-Renault. The line was massing behind her, not some pensioner-magician.

Kančeli couldn't possibly have known it was Elza, how could he? Anyway, his instincts had completely failed him when it came to Elza. Not a state employee, never wore a FUCK OFF button when she was young (and if he had gotten a better look at her in the carwash, he would have seen she was still youthful), and not at all the type of woman to carry an expensive purse. You've figured out already that Kančeli has come out looking like an idiot here. But he obstinately refused to reconsider his scenario.

She's really short, Kančeli thought as he looked her over. *Not tiny, short. Little bitty. Mrs. Little Bitty Blonde, LBB.* Not even the high-heeled sandals helped, she still had to get up on her tiptoes to sign the receipt at the counter. In her left hand (slender, frail, translucent fingers, like the tentacles of some bug), she held bundles of crisp new 200-Euro bills. *There's no way she's connected to a ministry or anything like that*, thought Kančeli, *no way at all*. She looked more like the wife of some mid-level criminal, or, more likely, the wife of some trades-man. But not the kind who helped her husband out in the shop, she didn't work anywhere, that was for sure. Someone who works doesn't wave money like that all over the place. People would cut your hand off these days for less than that. And that hand really was tempting, with what seemed like a billion Euros spread out in it like a peacock's tail.

Elza finished her business and left the bank. Kančeli followed her. Followed her because he'd never in his life seen anyone with so much cash in her pocket. Wondered what a half hour would be like in the life of someone with so much cash. As he walked behind her, he exhausted all the possible combinations he could make with her initials. Leering bombed Bolshevik. Last bombastic boozer. Licentious babbling bumblebee. And so forth, until they crossed the sidewalk and then through the parking lot to the Asterisk pizzeria. Elza sat down at a table in the corner and began to study the menu.

Kančeli sat at the other end of the pizzeria and studied her. Now that he'd gotten accustomed to her, she didn't seem so irritatingly short anymore. As far as her proportions were concerned, everything was perfectly in place, and especially the breasts—perky little pre-silicone contrivances the size of a fist, the nipples poking out from a menthol-green, cotton t-shirt.

Meanwhile, Kančeli was interrupted in his detailed observation of Elza because she had picked up on his inquiring gaze, gotten up, and come over to his table.

"Okay," she said, not bothering to disguise her animosity, "who are you? Some sexual maniac? A robber or something?"

Kančeli studied her with interest, as though he had standing in front of him an animal the likes of which he had never seen, never knew existed. Actually, Elza did resemble an animal with those frail, transparent finger-tentacles, the blonde, bristly tufts of hair, the jutted-out chin, the lips spewing poison.

"Or maybe you just want your mommy and that's why you've been running after me."

"You ought to call me 'sir'," Kančeli said, after thinking about it for a few seconds. "Considering the circumstances, you ought to be addressing me as 'sir.' A bumpkin like you running around with millions in your purse, thinking that gives you the right to talk to people that way."

Elza eased up a little, letting down her guard.

"And while we're on the subject, since when exactly have I been following you?" Kančeli asked, feeling like he'd taken the lead.

"I don't know, over there, since I left the bank," said Elza, confused.

"Oh no," Kančeli said, "you're wrong about that, we've known each other longer than that. That is, we almost met yesterday, missed it by a hair."

Elza seemed even more confused now.

"Which didn't prevent me from washing your car," Kančeli continued, "over at the car wash."

Elza was cautiously sizing him up.

"I didn't notice you there," she said.

"It doesn't matter," Kančeli said. "It's not a fashion runway. We're supposed to be invisible over there, but efficient. In the best of cases, on the same level as the big shampoo brushes. Satisfied with the cleaning? Any complaints? Please come again!"

Elza was stuck. The animosity she'd felt toward him earlier had completely disappeared.

"In short," Kančeli concluded, "I'm not a maniac or some kind of homeless person, and I don't want to take your money. I'm just the guy who washed your car."

Elza smiled. Her smile revealed a series of weathered, but attractive teeth. She looked over this garrulous man, thinking he didn't seem at all like a car washer (if there was such a thing as a stereotypical car washer) and had no criminal features.

"Although," Kančeli said, "while we were over on the sidewalk, it did occur to me to steal your purse. It's not a good idea to wave that much money in front of people's noses and then walk around with it."

"Can I sit down?" she asked.

"Sure," Kančeli said, "just don't forget your safe-deposit box," he said, gesturing over toward her purse.

She went for the purse, which had probably cost four hundred kuna or so, and returned to Kančeli's table.

"Elza," she said, and put out her hand.

Beli and Jajo were glued to the pizzeria window, giving them a significant look, and then Jajo, catching Kančeli's eye, raised his thumb in the air.

When he got home later, Kančeli spotted Čombe stretched out on the couch. "Well, I'm glad you like it so well here," he said.

Čombe raised his head and gave him a squinty look.

"Strange things are happening to me these days," Kančeli continued. "First, I keep forgetting to buy a container of gas, so now I can't make us any tea. And second, I keep meeting people with short names. Suzi, Elza—it's probably only a matter of seconds till some Ena or whatever bursts through the door. What do you think, huh? And do you consider it normal for this Elza to be walking around the neighborhood with a pile of money like that in her purse? Say whatever you like, but that's pretty suspicious to me."

Elza entered her empty apartment, shook the money onto the floor, and sat down among the bundles. Looked at the money and thought: *so, this is what all the time I've spent in this apartment is worth, everything I've experienced. Like in that fucking film when the guy tries to figure out the weight of cigarette smoke. Apartments are like boxes we just burn out in. This money, ashes are worth just as much; but how much is smoke worth?* And then she started crying, but not because of what once had been. She was crying about what could have been and wasn't, and she would put it all out of her mind as soon as she was able to calm down. So she got undressed and went into the shower, thinking as the droplets hit her skin about the car wash guy who didn't look like a car wash guy. Who actually didn't look bad at all.

25. The missing lighters and little Red Riding Hood's bodyguard

"Ah, and closing your eyes to it obviously doesn't help," said Baba, stopping in front of the statue of Prince Krsto Frankopan on Zrinjevac Park.

He'd just heard something he didn't like at all. It wasn't unexpected, what he'd heard. He knew it would catch up with him sooner or later and hit him right smack in the heart, but he played dumb. For a long time, he hadn't wanted to admit what was so obvious, or understand what was so understandable. Kančeli had come right out with it. Interrupted Baba right in the middle of his elegy about cars that disappeared and plastic lighters. Baba was complaining that when he got drunk, it was becoming increasingly hard to find his car. Forgot where he'd parked it. Sometimes it would be days before he would come across his Opel, just by chance while walking around town.

That's why the two of them were walking along Zrinjevac, looking for Baba's car, because Baba was one hundred percent sure he'd left it around here somewhere. It was the same thing with the plastic lighters. He had one once that advertised some café in Pazin, with the letter "S" worn off its name. And then the lighter just disappeared. Just like that. Someone took it off the table, put it in his pocket, and that was that.

"That summer," Baba said, "I found some work in Jezera on Murter. I'm drinking coffee in the café by the marina and realize my lighter's gone. I bum a light from the waiter, and he, like, pulls out, guess what?"

"Your lighter," Kančeli said.

"Yeah," said Baba, not at all surprised that Kančeli had anticipated the ending of the lighter escapade. "The lighter with that "S" missing. Imagine, these things just disappear and suddenly show up again where you least expect it."

And Kančeli blurted out without thinking: "Vera wants you to move out."

Kančeli stopped in front of the stone statue, confronted with the horrific face of the Croatian aristocrat. Krsto Frankopan, as everyone knows, died in 1527, but the expression on his face indicates he has just become aware of that fact.

"Check him out," Baba said, "he looks like he just had a vision of his own death."

"So," Kančeli said, "now we're going to talk about Frankopan, huh? What does fucking Frankopan have to do with what I just told you?"

"Look at that one over there," Baba said, pointing to another statue.

"Unbelievable," said Kančeli.

"Ivan Mažuranić," said Baba. "Look how he's sulking, like a snot-nosed kid. His back turned to Frankopan, sulking—and you know why? Because the Mažuranićs were Frankopan's tenants, that's why. And that haunted him his whole life. But he was a serf in his soul. 'You're not great just because you were born to greatness, you're greater if you were born into nothing,' as Mažuranić said. Don't give me your fucking homespun wisdom. Just because you're on the street doesn't make you great, but being in Parliament does—Fuck off!"

"I don't need this."

Baba relaxed immediately.

"No problem, bro," he said, taking Kančeli under his arm. "Everything's clear to me; I just don't like hearing it."

Two policemen with Kalashnikovs over their shoulders were standing in front of the Ministry of Foreign Affairs.

"Well of course," Baba said, as he looked them over. "Little Red Riding Hoods are working inside, and they need to protect them from the two of us and all the other wolves out on the streets."

"What's the problem?" Kančeli asked.

Baba looked Kančeli in the eye.

"Seems like I'm the problem," he said. "I'm fucked, man. Totally fucked. I've been acting like an idiot for years—I don't know exactly what I want, but I've definitely been looking for it in all the wrong places. You know? I tell myself every night: okay, you imbecile, starting tomorrow, you're going to do things differently. Either you'll act like a human being or pack up and leave Vera."

They crossed the street under the watchful eyes of the police.

"And now it's all over," said Baba dryly. "Over, way past over. Fuck it. I think I parked over in that direction," he said, pointing west, and then he looked over at the policemen. "You're doing a great job, boys. I'm satisfied; keep up the good work."

26. Don't look in Samobor for what you can find in Utrine

These little towns where nothing happens, where births, weddings, and deaths are the major news items, they're so small when you're looking for some kind of entertainment, but megalopolises when you try to locate one particular person. So, Stjepan intended to find Magda in Samobor. Seen from some pilotless spy satellite, his journey looked like this: he took off on some crooked, spirally route starting from the marketplace, whizzed down some windy little streets and crossed a bridge that took him to a cemetery on the hill, and then to the old train station, the barracks, the lumber warehouse, and then wound back to the starting point.

He kept getting lost along these little streets, couldn't find his way north from most of the spots, but still he kept on walking. He'd be surprised every time he'd come to a spot from which he could find his way back to the main square or the marketplace.

Except for Magda's name and description, all other elements that were important when conducting a search were unknown to Stjepan. His chances of finding Magda were extremely slim, he'd known that at the outset, but he'd taken heart from the fact that the city was so small, luckily, (though we know luck's not exactly one of his close friends), and that Magda had the habit of going to the marketplace every day.

So, he assumed he would sooner or later run into her at the marketplace. If she was caring for her daughter, then it was an absolutely logical conclusion that she would show up at the marketplace. But she didn't. And she didn't show up at the bakery, either, where Stjepan had purchased a poppy bun he'd eaten on the way. And she wasn't on the old, wooden bridge, or the walkway along the river. She wasn't in any of the little streets or avenues Stjepan had been weaving through like a rabid dog for most of the morning. And she wasn't on the terrace at noon when he stopped to rest, to have a spritzer and smoke a Sumatran cigarillo. He wasn't in the mood for either one.

These little villages can be interesting when you're there purely as a tourist, to have a coffee and a cream cake or something. But when you're there on business, especially delicate business like finding a missing person, then they get on your last nerve. As the day went on and the search brought no results whatsoever, Stjepan began to feel revulsion toward Samobor. First, animosity, then revulsion, and finally loathing. *The layout of the town is so ridiculous*, he growled to himself. *Everything in the wrong place, as though the streets were plotted out by some lunatic; otherwise they wouldn't twist and turn like this. Fuck, a town that has fewer inhabitants than my neighborhood!* Utrine was a metropolis compared to Samobor.

His gorge rose at the thought of Samobor, thinking he could raze it to the ground, with all its bridges and baroque bullshit, and his conscience wouldn't bother him an iota.

He returned to Zagreb in this frame of mind. And when the bus reached Jankomir Bridge, and he saw the chimney of the heating plant rising out of the filthy smog in the east, Stjepan's heart skipped a beat. *Blessed Utrine*, he thought, *where the streets all intersect at right angles, where everything is where it's supposed to be. All except Magda.*

There's an old Utrine proverb that goes like this: don't go to Samobor for what you can find in Utrine.

Late that afternoon, climbing the stairs up to the entrance to his apartment building (still loathing Samobor), he saw Magda getting out of the elevator. Anger, the first thing he articulated was anger. "Well, where in the hell have you been, woman?" And then self-pity. "I almost lost my life stumbling around that lousy village." Then joy. "Magda, I'm so fucking glad to see you." Finally censure. "Why didn't you tell me you were leaving? All kinds of things went through my head when you took off like that."

Magda waited patiently while Stjepan let off steam, and then said, "I rang the bell downstairs, but nobody was home."

"You could have called from Samobor."

"How?"

"What do you mean, how? On the phone."

"I don't have your number," Magda said calmly, "you were the one who always called."

Stjepan hung his head, suddenly noticing something very interesting on the ground.

Žac and Beli were passing by the building. "Check Štef out," Beli said. "He probably screwed up somehow, and now he's trying to figure out how to get out of it."

27. How it ended

It was close to noon when Suzi crawled out of bed, put on her cotton t-shirt with the Barbie-as-a-prostitute design which hung down to mid-thigh (Suzi's mother had a hard time with designs and t-shirt lengths, so the fashion disasters she got from her, Suzi mostly wore around the house), and took a look at the boy sleeping in her bed. He was lying on his back, hands under his head, breathing quietly and deeply. *Shit, he's still a baby; I could get in trouble with the cops because of him.*

She picked him up last night in the Seven bar. He was pretty lost in there, gave up without a fight; it had been enough just to gesture over to him from the other side of the bar that she needed a cigarette. And now she watched as he slept here, like some child. Suzi felt better than she'd felt in a very long time. No vestiges of filth on her skin which could not be removed even after a long shower (the frequent result of a one-night stand), no feeling of discomfort sticking to the skin like grease. On the contrary, she felt butterflies in her stomach and had the inclination to laugh. *What was his name again?* she asked herself. *Marko? Mario?* It doesn't matter. Whatever his name was, he worked on her like an Alka-Seltzer after a particularly bad party.

Suzi had really felt hungover in recent days. No, she hadn't gotten wasted at parties, hadn't been drinking at all; it was just the complicated story with Robi and Vera that had messed up her head.

Why had Vera invented that thing about pornography? Why had she told her all that stuff about Robi and his mother? Why had Vera sucked her into her own private hell? Suzi was confused by it all, and began to avoid Vera. She didn't know what to think. Was Vera nice or disgusting? Life isn't black and white, that's obvious, but some colors have to dominate, some tones. Which tone dominated with Vera? What game was she playing?

And then, one day in the city, Suzi ran into that weirdo Kančeli, and over drinks found out that Robi really wasn't a victim of a monstrous mother.

"No, that has nothing to do with it," Kančeli said, "Vera's exaggerating. He is a little too dependent on his parents, especially his mother, but who isn't dependent on something these days? We don't have to take him out behind the barn and shoot him because of that," Kančeli said.

He added that Robi was just a rich kid trying to play proletariat and writer, and having little success at either. And then reminded her that Vera didn't like Robi because he'd dumped a good friend of hers a long time ago, who'd then taken a bunch of pills, stuck her head in a gas oven, and so forth. "She didn't kill herself, of course," Kančeli concluded, "she never meant to, but Sylvia Plath was in fashion then, you know?"

Then Suzi asked herself why she'd even believed she and Vera could become close. *I was so stupid. It's like I wanted to get close to my mother.* And then all of a sudden she saw Vera in a different light. A woman who'd made a mess of her life. A very lonely woman. Suzi didn't exclude the possibility that something similar might be awaiting her in the future, some similar shit, but she definitely wasn't hurrying in that direction. Why should she? Aging is a one-way street, and despite all the tricks of plastic surgery, you can't drive back in the same direction.

Vera's observation that she knew what it was like to be Suzi's age, but would Suzi ever know what it would be like to be Vera's age, was a question that assumed new significance. Suzi now interpreted the observation as envy instead of wisdom.

Maybe you're right, Suzi thought, *but the chances are very good that I will reach famous fucking middle age one day, while there's no possibility at all that you will ever again return to your twenties.* So she stopped answering the telephone, and when she heard Vera's voice on the machine, she would think: *no thanks. Please don't liberate me from my age anymore; I've decided to take complete pleasure in it.*

And now, as Suzi drank her coffee, the telephone rang. She sipped her coffee as she listened to Vera's electronic voice: "Hey, lost daughter, this is a perfect day to go for a coffee."

"Who is that? Your mom?"

Suzi turned around. At the door stood her trophy from the night before.

"Something like that," she said.

She gestured for him to sit down at the table and asked him if he wanted a regular Nescafé or one with milk.

Meanwhile, Robi's yellow vw was circling around Louisiana. With a tank full of unleaded gas, you could go to the end of the world and back again. But Robi wasn't driving around the world, only to the island of Krk. He was in no hurry to get there. Driving and acting cool, eyes hidden behind sunglasses, an open can of beer in his right hand. Pretending that he had no idea where he was headed, but wherever it was, he didn't want to get there on the new highway to Rijeka. He was driving through old Louisiana, chugging the beer. All sorts of things were going through his mind. That he was the last remaining member of the *On the Road* gang. The only legitimate successor to Jack Kerouac. That he'd just set out for Paris where Zadie Smith was waiting for him, and then they'd head for Tangier—things like that. "That's right, the old road for an old fucker," he mumbles into his beard.

"Speed is inappropriate at my age, young man," he says to a boy selling mushrooms along the street.

"No destination on earth is worth speeding for, you moron," he says to the guy who passes him.

"Life consists solely of chasing your own tail," he says to the trees at the side of the road.

"Walk through life with slow, elegant steps, like a black panther," says Robi to his sunglasses and forehead in the rearview mirror.

And since he wanted company, and couldn't just slough off that last encounter with Baba, he put together the following scenario: he had just picked up Baba, his immigrant piece-of-shit Opel had overheated and died in the middle of the road, and Robi stops and generously offers to drive Baba to the nearest mechanic. Baba accepts gratefully, and now the two are driving ahead. In the Yellow Streak.

Pretty good, huh? Robi says, just to get the conversation going.

Well, it's definitely not a '56 Chevy, says Baba jealously.

Cut the bullshit, Robi says, *this isn't Route 66.*

The motor, injected with synthetic oil, started to growl menacingly in anticipation of the kilometers of asphalt that lay ahead.

Listen to it growl, says Robi, giving it gas as they came out of the curve.

Growl! Baba says in amazement. *Can you even say for a car like this that it's growling?*

Robi slams on the brakes and the car spins out in the dirt, coming to a stop at the side of the road.

Out! Robi says, pointing with his index finger toward the mountain peaks in the distance.

Why? Baba asks.

Because you're full of shit, Robi says. *Why can't you say for a vw that it growls?* Robi got dangerously into Baba's face.

Because a vw isn't a Maserati or anything like it, Baba says, *that's why.*

There was a distance of two inches between their noses.

Get the hell out, Robi says.

We're not going to duke it out now, are we? says Baba, meanwhile realizing that Robi's not kidding.

Besides, says Robi, *since when do you care about labels; you get your clothes at the flea market.*

I didn't say I cared about labels, says Baba, *I just said a vw wasn't a Maserati.*

Take a hike, says Robi.

And Baba disappears from the car, and Robi is alone again.

And since it was really boring driving alone, Robi conjured up a girl at a truck stop, thumb in the air. Suzi, it was fucking Suzi.

Hop in, Robi says suavely, *the road awaits us.*

I love your wheels, says Suzi, kissing Robi on the lips.

You do?

Yeah, a lot, says Suzi. *Yours is different from all the other vws in the world, it's unique, one and only, there's no vw in the world like it.*

Robi pressed down on the gas pedal, and the forest changed into a green blur.

And you know what makes it so unique?

Tell me.

You're driving it, says Suzi. *Every day it takes on your qualities, from the rhythm of your movements, to all your little idiosyncrasies. And all your elegance, eccentricity, and so forth, it's permeated the lacquer of this car and made it so elegant and eccentric.*

Robi cried out and now really slammed on the brakes, and the car came to a stop in a cloud of dust at the edge of the road.

"What the fuck is the matter with you, you idiot!" yelled the guy who'd been driving behind and laying on the horn. "You want to get us all killed?"

And Robi didn't hear the yelling or the horn. He didn't hear anything, only his own heart beating madly. He rested his head on the steering wheel, thinking life was a bitch.

And Kančeli and Elza are lying in a little room whose walls are covered with children's drawings. The work of Kančeli's daughter. The scribblings in which parents recognize the future genius of their offspring, and psychiatrists the grotesqueness of their present existence.

Kančeli wasn't that type of parent. He hadn't even noticed the drawings until the two had deserted him. His wife had, for some reason, left them on the wall. Took everything out of the rooms, down to the last speck of dust, but left the drawings. Kančeli had thought about getting rid of them the same day he'd gotten rid of the cup with those stupid cows painted on it, but he hadn't. He left them on the wall as a reminder that the room with the drawings had for a long time been the museum of his bad conscience. But that had changed. Now it was just an ordinary room hung with a child's scribblings, in which Elza and Kančeli were lying on the mattress covered with an unzipped sleeping bag. Kančeli, holding Elza's hand in his, was staring at the ceiling and listening to her talk.

Elza was talking about her honeymoon in Halkidiki, the fields of sunflowers and the huge green snakes on the peninsula, and the silver Citroen Igor and she had bought on credit which she kept paying after he had died, the closure of the shop she had worked in, the last vacation they'd taken together to Mljet, the lobsters in the restaurant on the lake, and how Igor didn't want to even hear about leaving the brigade until the war was over, how they planned to go to New Zealand, how she found a job in Vienna through the owner of the kiosk she worked in, but that she wasn't sure if it was really in a nursing home or something else, and how she had gone with Igor to the barracks that day, and a black cat had crossed their path, similar to the one today, here in front of the apartment building.

She rambled on, weeping.

And then, Kančeli talked about the parties that Irene (he spoke the name he never mentioned in front of others for the first time in a long while) loved to organize, and how she'd changed after Maja was born, how she'd retreat into her room every time he'd come home with friends, his wild drinking, rowdy fistfights, the broken windows and counters, his yelling at Irene every time she'd object to his drinking, the cup with the cows, the shrink with the hawk-like face and visions in the hospital park, people with eyes of dead fish, and that the cat she'd seen in front of the building was only Čombe, a friendly cat, she shouldn't worry... He spoke and spoke, squeezing her hand tightly.

By talking to each other like this, they shed their own past. They talked and looked somewhere beyond the walls, trembling, as though a cold moon and not the blazing summer sun was hitting against the glass and cement of the high-rise.

At about the same time, Baba is holding out to Vera the keys to the apartment, saying he's going to come for the books and other things sometime in the fall, if that's okay.

"That's fine," said Vera.

"But of course I'll call first," he said and lifted his sports bag from the floor.

"Yes, be sure to," Vera said.

"I rented something downtown," he said, turning toward the door. "Some dive."

"Good," Vera said.

"See you," he said, closing the door behind him.

Vera remained standing in the hall, the keys in her hand. When the sound of Baba's footsteps faded away, she put the keys on the dresser, went into the kitchen, and washed out the cup from which Baba had drunk his coffee. Then she called Suzi. The last few days she'd only gotten Suzi's answering machine. Just like now. Vera left a message, then sat down and tried to figure out what to do. Go to the coast, visit Duda in London, write an essay on new women's British prose, organize her closet, throw out clothes she hasn't worn for years, write Tom, get drunk, lie down and sleep through the summer...

So many plans were whirling around in her head. She thought about how good a cigarette would taste right now, how it would settle things in her head, but it seemed stupid to immediately replace Baba with another bad habit. She tried to name what she felt. Was it relief? She took off her too-tight Italian-fucking-shoes. Or was it Spanish boots.

Vera imagined that after a long bus ride that stank of sweat and gas, she had reached a little town in the mountains, and was standing on a tiled square in front of a church, a breeze blew down from the mountains, and all the time in the world was hers.

Nothing felt right to her. What she felt was suffocation. As though she were riding in a packed elevator, all the bodies pressed together, and she couldn't move, started to panic. She had to get out of the apartment. Yes, that's what she'd do. A half hour later, she rang the doorbell to an apartment on the first floor of an apartment building on Deželić Alley.

"Hi, Mom," she said and kissed the woman who opened the door.

"So," said Vera's mother, putting a teapot on the table a few minutes later, "you got into another fight with Baba."

"Why do you think that?" Vera asked.

"Because the only time you come over is when you fight."

"It's not like that," Vera said. "And we didn't get in a fight; we're just not together anymore."

Her mother didn't seem surprised about what she heard. She just looked at Vera, trying to read what was written in her eyes.

"Is it because of the drinking?" she asked finally.

"Where'd that come from?" said Vera, taking a sip of tea from the porcelain cup.

Vera's mother had inherited the tea service from her mother, who had bought it in some antique shop in Amsterdam, and if the story were true, the service came to Holland in the first shipment of tea from China. Vera had heard the story many times and didn't really believe it. But she did like drinking tea from the porcelain cups that had traveled all around the world to end up in her hands. They gave the tea a special flavor, just like those sugared fruits.

"What else could it be," her mother said. "He's not the type who goes through a second puberty. Both of you have had, shall we say, a long and tempestuous youth."

Vera remained silent.

"Drink can pull a man down," said her mother, "it just grabs you. And Baba, as far as I know, was never able to resist things like that."

"Baba never got to that phase, mama," Vera said. "You're right, he doesn't run from the bottle, that's no secret, but that still doesn't mean he's in a phase where it presents a serious problem. In any case," she said putting the cup down on the table, "alcohol's not the reason Baba and I split up."

"Then what is the reason?" her mother asked.

Vera got up and approached the cabinet on which the framed portrait of her father was displayed. She smelled the photograph and could have sworn she detected the scent of his cologne water. Vera couldn't stand that smell because it reminded her of traveling by car, and as a child, she'd been carsick. Every time her father woke her up at dawn, smelling of cologne water, Vera knew she'd be spending that day in a car heading toward the coast and that she'd be throwing up. Later, when puberty had resolved her carsickness, Vera's stomach would still turn at the scent of cologne water.

"We tired of each other, I guess," said Vera, holding back her nausea. "Or else it's some little thing I didn't notice in Baba before—something that didn't bother me before. Maybe he uses the wrong aftershave, or holds his cigarette in an irritating manner, I don't know."

"Your father and I—" her mother began.

"I know, Mama," Vera interrupted, "you went through a lot of crises together, helping one another, you never gave up, and so forth, until death do you part, his death," she said, pointing at his portrait, "but I don't want to get into that now. I didn't come for advice; I just came to tell you and to have tea with you, okay?"

Her mother shrugged her shoulders.

"Then do you want to move in here?" she asked, knowing in advance what she would hear.

"No," Vera smiled. "Baba's already moved out."

And Baba was lying in a ground-level room facing the courtyard in an apartment building on Medulić Street, thinking about the literature of the first half of the twentieth century. Why had that come to mind? First, he was overcome with dejection after scanning the tiny apartment and realizing he was going to spend who knows how many days, months, or years in it. Compared to this rented apartment, Kančeli's cement cave—which usually gave him the creeps—seemed entirely acceptable. Then he experienced an attack of paramnesia. Fucking déjà vu. He knew this place; he knew it well. The strong odor of dampness, the bulging carpet stained with gray and brown spots (like an old naval map), furniture with the finish peeling off, a sparse kitchen separated from the living room by a faded curtain, a communal bathroom down the hall with an iron sink and yellowed, cracked mirror. And the courtyard overgrown with weeds, a cafeteria, and a mechanic's workshop full of broken axles, motors, and all sorts of other auto parts.

Baba had read about such places in stories by writers at the beginning of the previous century and asked himself what he had done to deserve reliving the past in such a manner.

He woke up at dusk with a headache. He sat at the edge of the bed, and it took him awhile to figure out where he was. And figuring out where he was didn't make anything easier. A song about the soul, heart, and eyes emanated from the cafeteria.

He got up and went to the refrigerator. It was a real old-timer. He felt the cans of beer lined up inside. Right away, he felt better. And his headache subsided a bit. He took out a beer and a bottle of vodka. In the cabinet above the sink, he found a stubby mug of brushed glass. He put everything on the table and got to work. *To the Slavonian soul, vodka and beer. To the wounded heart, vodka and beer. To the jet-black eyes, vodka and beer. To the cracked carburetor blocks, vodka and beer.* He got up and went for a new can of beer. *To the vodka and beer. To Mažuranić and all the other serfs, vodka and fuckinggoodbeer. To the old refrigerator, vodka and beer. To the landlord's dentures, vodka and beer. To you, my friend,* as he raised the glass toward the shadow that passed in front of the window, *vodka and beer.*

Baba chugged down as much as he could. He was always able to drink a lot, but now his sorrow increased his capacity. It was after midnight and all sound had ceased from the cafeteria when Baba realized he had nothing more to drink. And he was still going strong; the booze had hardly affected him. He sat for a while staring into the dark courtyard.

Then he dragged himself to the bed, lay down, buried his head and fists in the pillow, and began to cry. He wailed like a dog. Then he got up, went to the bathroom, and pissed. Blew his nose, washed his face, and ran his wet fingers through his hair. He was not discouraged by what he saw in the mirror. He was not ashamed of the red eyes and the burst blood vessels.

Who gives a fuck, he thought, *none of this is true. I've just fallen into some ancient, bizarre tale. Tomorrow everything will be fine.*

He crept back into bed and fell asleep.

28. What happened afterward

This is a story with a happy ending. As Cendrars said: being sad is too easy, too stupid, too comfortable, not clever, and always attainable.

Baba no longer suffers from the fear of going home. He has settled down in this little apartment on Medulić Street, he's writing some things, puttering around in the auto shop learning how to fix motors, and in the evening, he brings a chair out into the courtyard, sits there, smokes, contemplates life with Vera and various other things, and thinks how long ago it all was.

And begins to realize how stupid it is to live alone. The other day he had to ask the waiter to apply hydrogen drops to his stuffed-up ear.

And how much sweat it cost him to take care of that ugly pimple on his back!

And what other ridiculous situations he had never thought of before awaited him?

In the morning, he's up in the marketplace, sitting in one of those cafés, drinking coffee, people-watching, and writing things in his notebook. He still hasn't gone to Vera's for his things. *There's plenty of time*, he thinks, *summer's just begun. Something is sure to happen by then, or not.*

When he thinks about drinking, and this is often, very often, he tells himself: *tomorrow, man, hang one on tomorrow; the moon is in its first quarter today, and that's a bad sign.* He often runs into Vera's mother in town. They go for a coffee, talk about the weather, how this and that has gotten more expensive, and so on. And she asks him every time why Vera and he broke up, and he says every time: "All that matters is that we're alive and healthy."

"I'm so sorry about the two of you," she then says.

"So am I, ma'am, so am I."

Vera thought all the weight would fall from her when Baba left. That she'd wake up in the morning refreshed, stretch, roll her eyes, and begin to experience everything again for the first time. And she was right. All the details connected to the taste of coffee were new, a tingling in her palate she'd never before experienced. Then she'd put on a Björk CD and listen to the heavenly-demonic sounds, a whole scale of sounds that could otherwise be heard only with the assistance of drugs.

Then she'd buy an eggplant at the marketplace, fry it, and read Cendrars' *Prose of the Trans-Siberian* as she ate, imagining herself each time Jeanne would ask: "Blaise, tell me, are we far from Montmartre?" But, she would still get the shivers when she'd hear the sound of the elevator doors. She'd be all ears for a few moments, listening breathlessly to the footsteps in the hall, only exhaling when they stopped in front of another door, when the key slipped into another lock.

And Suzi finally answered the phone. "I'm sorry I stuck my nose into your life," Vera told her. Suzi was silent on the other end of the line. Vera hung up, mumbling, "You cold little bitch, you're going to go really far in life."

Once she dreamt of Tom. That he was bald, with those lines around the eyes and a beer belly. They had run into each other on Flower Square, the way it used to be, right in front of that old water pump. Stood there and looked at each other. They weren't surprised, didn't get excited over seeing each other again. There was no scene. They were just a little stunned. Like they were continuing the dream in a waking state, calm, in slow motion, like marijuana smokers. They still e-mail each other, because the Internet is faster than the mail and cheaper than a shrink.

Kančeli got a job as a waiter at the Asterisk. It didn't take him long to get used to being on the wrong side of the counter. It was a little more difficult getting used to the electric stove, telephone, television, and all the other loud objects in the apartment. Plus, all the furniture.

"I come only with the whole package," Elza told him. Kančeli had no other choice. Sometimes he felt as though these things around him were stealing his air, beginning to suffocate him. Then he'd take his camp stove, go out onto the balcony, and make some tea, and then Elza would join him, drink tea with him, and they'd talk about the future. They didn't discuss any spectacular plans. Just what they were going to have for lunch the next day, what film they'd go see, whether they'd go hiking on Sljeme or Japetić on Sunday.

Baba visited them at least once a week. They sat in the living room, invited Stjepan over, and then Baba would read them his stories. Afterward they'd give their comments, and Baba would stoically consider the various critical observations. Once, Kančeli asked him if he'd like to invite Vera next time. Baba stared at some spot on the wall.

"So you think," he said after a long moment, "that it's possible to have your cake and eat it, too."

"No, it's not, but that doesn't mean I can't look at the cake once in a while," said Kančeli.

"I agree," said Baba, "but you're forgetting that people aren't goddamn cakes."

Stjepan gave his telephone number to Magda. He gave it to her the night he returned from Samobor. It signaled significant changes in their relationship, but Magda still needed quite a while to adjust to the following situation:

"Hi, Magda, it's Štef."

"I'm on my way."

"No, Magda, I'm calling to ask you if you'd like to go out for a pastry with me. I really feel like a Sachertorte."

On the other hand, Magda wasn't a bit amused when she would call him about something else, and he would say: "I'm sorry, Magda, but my little guy is a bit depressed today. How about tomorrow?" Or some other similar nonsense.

And the girls in the video store were concerned for a while that Stjepan was no longer renting pornos.

"Too bad he can't get it up anymore, he's such a nice old guy," they said. Later, they stopped thinking about it completely.

Robi moved out of his parents' house. He rented an apartment in the Dubrava district and began to live off the bookstore. He patiently repeated to his mother, who was constantly hovering around the bookstore urging him to move back home, "That house is not my home."

Suzi continued to devour her youth. Her conscience bothered her a bit about the way she'd blown Vera off, but just a bit, because she felt Vera wouldn't really hold her lack of compassion against her. Compassion came with age, right? She got a role in the pilot of some series. The script was inane, but that didn't bother her. She thought: *give me anything at all, a telephone book, and I'll put my whole heart into it.*

And Čombe continued to shuttle back and forth between Stjepan and Kančeli. They didn't mind. And neither did he.

About the author

EDO POPOVIĆ was born in 1957 in Livno, Bosnia and Herzegovina. He has lived in Zagreb since 1968. He was one of the founders and editors of the literary magazine *Quorum*. His fiction, reviews, reportage, and articles have been published in major magazines, political weeklies, and daily papers. His previous books include *Dream of Yellow Snakes* (2000), *Concert for Tequila and Prozac* (2002), and *A Dancer from the Blue Bar* (2004). His fiction has been featured in various anthologies and has been translated into German, English, and Slovenian. His novella *Dream of Yellow Snakes* was translated and dramatized by Canadian theater director Danijel Margetić for Reeve Secondary Theatre in Calgary.

Ooligan Press

Ooligan Press takes its name from a Native American word for the common smelt or candlefish. Ooligan is a general trade press rooted in the rich literary life of Portland and the Department of English at Portland State University. Ooligan is staffed by students pursuing master's degrees in an apprenticeship program under the guidance of a core faculty of publishing professionals.

OOLIGAN PRESS TEAM
Project manager: Olivia Koivisto
Cover design: Alan Dubinsky
Interior design: Meredith Norwich, assisted by Linda Meyer
Senior editors: Dave Cowsert, Olivia Koivisto, and Linda Meyer
Proofreading: Linda Meyer, Rebekah Hunt
Marketing: Olivia Koivisto, Meredith Norwich

ASSISTANCE PROVIDED BY:
Susan Applegate
Lake Boggan
Sean Conners
Laura Dewing
Jay M. Evans
Karen Kirtley
Sharon Helms
Ali McCart
Marian Paul
Aimee Shelton
Dennis Stovall

OOLIGAN
P R E S S

Post Office Box 751
Portland, Oregon 97207
Phone: 503.725.9748 | Fax: 503.725.3561
ooligan@ooliganpress.pdx.edu | www.ooliganpress.pdx.edu

Ooligan Press is a general trade publisher rooted in the rich literary tradition of the Pacific Northwest. A region widely recognized for its unique and innovative sensibilities, this small corner of America is one of the most diverse in the United States, comprising urban centers, small towns, and wilderness areas. Its residents range from ranchers, loggers, and small business owners to scientists, inventors, and corporate executives. From this wealth of culture, Ooligan Press aspires to discover works that reflect the values and attitudes that inspire so many to call the Northwest their home.

Founded in 2001, Ooligan is a teaching press dedicated to the art and craft of publishing. Affiliated with Portland State University, the press is staffed by students pursuing master's degrees in an apprenticeship program under the guidance of a core faculty of publishing professionals.

Ordering information

Individual Sales: All Ooligan Press titles are available through your local bookstore, and we encourage supporting independent booksellers. Please contact your local bookstore, or purchase online through Powell's, Indiebound, or Amazon.

Retail Sales: Ooligan books are distributed to the trade through Ingram Publisher Services (IPS). Booksellers and businesses that wish to stock Ooligan titles may order directly from IPS at (866) 400-5351 or customerservice@ingrampublisherservices.com.

Educational and Library Sales: We sell directly to educators and libraries that do not have an established relationship with IPS. For pricing, or to place an order, please contact us at operations@ooliganpress.pdx.edu.

American Scream &
Palindrome Apocalype

Dubravka Oraić Tolić

poetry | 240 pages | $14.95
6" x 9" | softcover | ISBN: 978-1-932010-10-7

Utopia—we all want our own, but who pays for it and at what price? Croatian poet Dubravka Oraić Tolić's delivers a masterful, thought-provoking answer with exquisite language and imagery in the epic poem *American Scream.* As Columbus's dream of reaching India was interrupted by the discovery of a new land, we too discover unexpected lands in pursuit of our dreams.

Complementing *American Scream* is *Palindrome Apocalypse*—a palindrome that is artful in both technique and story—presented side-by-side with the Croatian original to preserve its visual effect.

> *Dubravka Oraić Tolić goes beyond playing with language and textual contexts. Although reality and notions of home, country, people, nation, and life permeate her poetry, the thematic weight does not rest on the semantic deconstruction of concrete geographical-historical localities, but on their empowerment through words, metaphors and symbols as elements of the text and culture.*
> — *Dr. Bernarda Katusić, University of Vienna*

Ooligan Press • Portland, Oregon • www.ooliganpress.pdx.edu

Do Angels Cry?

Tales of the War

Matko Marušić

fiction | 160 pages | $14.95

5½" x 8½" |softcover | ISBN: 978-1-932010-23-7

In 1991, war broke out in Croatia. Matko Marušić's short stories offer a human perspective on the war that is not told in history books. Each story illuminates the love and dedication the Croatian people have for their country, and their struggle to find purpose and meaning in the midst of tragedy. Matko Marušić's other writings include a novel, a collection of short stories for children, and two additional collections of short stories for adults. *Do Angels Cry? Tales of the War* was originally published in Croatia and Great Britain in 1996. A preface, written by Dr. Stanimir Vuk-Pavlovic, has been added for the American edition.

> *This book is about the facet of the human price of the war… Yet, this book tells the simple truth of the ordinary people caught in extraordinarily desperate situations when choices are few and all are bad. They are the response to the statement, "What is not worth dying for, is not worth living for." — Dr. Stanimir Vuk-Pavlovic*

Ooligan Press • Portland, Oregon • www.ooliganpress.pdx.edu

The Survival League

Gordan Nuhanović

fiction | 104 pages | $10.95

5½" x 8½" | softcover | ISBN: 978-1-932010-06-0

In *The Survival League*, Gordan Nuhanović delves past Croatia's post-war politics and focuses on its people struggling to heal old wounds and create new lives. With edgy, evocative prose, Nuhanović weaves darkly optimistic tales where nothing ever works out quite right: English lawns grow daisies instead of grass, and a romantic weekend in the mountains turns into a near-death experience. While war casts a shadow over all the characters, Nuhanović's use of everyday events and occurrences makes *The Survival League* ring true in any culture. Through Nuhanović's natural storytelling voice, we hear the stories of survivors, not only of war, but of life and its challenges. *The Survival League*'s humanity is universal, but a brief history of Croatia and an author's note about the origin of each story create a firm cultural context for the English-speaking world. The book is not only an ironic glimpse into the limits of human endurance but also a lesson in modern Croatian culture.

Already a hit in Croatia, *The Survival League* won the Society of Croatian Writers' Nightingale Award and the Ivan and Josip Kozarac Award. The Croatian daily newspaper *Jutarnji List* called it one of the top five books of 2002.

Ooligan Press • Portland, Oregon • www.ooliganpress.pdx.edu

Colophon

This manuscript was set in Adobe Caslon Pro, with titles in Legault.